THIS WILL ONLY TAKE A MINUTE

100 CANADIAN FLASHES

ESSENTIAL ANTHOLOGIES SERIES 16

Canada

ONTARIO ARTS COUNCIL
CONSEIL DES ARTS DE L'ONTARIO
an Ontario government agency
un organisme du gouvernement de l'Ontario

Canada Council for the Arts
Conseil des arts du Canada

Guernica Editions Inc. acknowledges the support
of the Canada Council for the Arts and the Ontario Arts Council.
The Ontario Arts Council is an agency of the Government of Ontario.
We acknowledge the financial support of the Government of Canada.

THIS WILL ONLY TAKE A MINUTE

100 CANADIAN FLASHES

Edited by
Bruce Meyer & Michael Mirolla

GUERNICA EDITIONS

TORONTO • CHICAGO • BUFFALO • LANCASTER (U.K.)
2022

Michael Mirolla & Connie McParland, general editors
Bruce Meyer & Michael Mirolla, editors
Cover and interior design: Rafael Chimicatti
Guernica Editions Inc.
287 Templemead Drive, Hamilton (ON), Canada L8W 2W4
2250 Military Road, Tonawanda, N.Y. 14150-6000 U.S.A.
www.guernicaeditions.com

Distributors:
Independent Publishers Group (IPG)
600 North Pulaski Road, Chicago IL 60624
University of Toronto Press Distribution (UTP)
5201 Dufferin Street, Toronto (ON), Canada M3H 5T8
Gazelle Book Services, White Cross Mills
High Town, Lancaster LA1 4XS U.K.

First edition.
Printed in Canada.

Legal Deposit – Third Quarter
Library of Congress Catalog Card Number: 2022934890
Library and Archives Canada Cataloguing in Publication
Title: This will only take a minute : Canadian flash fiction / compiled and edited by
Bruce Meyer & Michael Mirolla.
Names: Meyer, Bruce, 1957- editor. | Mirolla, Michael, 1948- editor.
Series: Essential anthologies series ; 16.
Description: Series statement: Essential anthologies series ; 16
Identifiers: Canadiana (print) 20220195986 | Canadiana (ebook) 20220196001
ISBN 9781771837514 (softcover) | ISBN 9781771837521 (EPUB)
Subjects: LCSH: Short stories, English—Canada.
LCSH: Canadian fiction—21st century. | CSH: Short stories, Canadian (English)
CSH: Canadian fiction (English)—21st century.
Classification: LCC PS8329.1 .T55 2022 | DDC C813/.010806—dc23

CONTENTS

Introduction: This Will Only Take a Minute

Flash fiction hasn't had the attention it deserves in Canada though that is beginning to change. The writers in this anthology are the new trailblazers for fiction in a nation renowned for its longer short stories. Long short stories are admirable. They only take an hour or two of one's time. Who has an hour or two to read a story?

Flash has been a form of fiction since the longer short story gained momentum. Anton Chekhov wrote vignettes and very short stories as well as short stories in the ten-thousand-word range. He was a busy man, a medical student who didn't have more than a few minutes to jot down his narratives. The same was true for Hemingway who lived with a journalist's deadlines and compressed reportage had to be telegraphed. He also had a busy social schedule.

Everyone has his or her reason for writing flash fiction. I began writing flash after suffering a severe concussion in a car accident. The brevity of a flash story helped me regain my command of language and ideas, and the redrafting portion of the work was a gift where I was able to remember words, phrases, and choose the right one in the right place. Writing flash stories is like hot air ballooning. The story flies better the more one tosses overboard.

Over the past decade, flash has gained tremendous popularity among authors, editors, and readers. A reader or an editor faces all manner of tugs on his or her time—social media, job demands, commuting, and family duties—and a little voice in their mind says, "Oh please, just tell me a story."

Flash is not easy to write. The shorter the story, the more the writer must concentrate on the art of compression, the detailed focus one finds in poetry, and the brevity that must embrace as many aspects of storytelling as longer works. From under a hundred words to five hundred, a good flash squeezes every drop of the short story into a small but exquisite space. Those whose work is represented in this anthology would agree that the two hundred word story is often more difficult and time-consuming to write than the two thousand word story.

Here, in this anthology, the writers follow Shakespeare's dictum that brevity is the soul of wit. Wit is not just about being funny. Wit is the intelligence of decision-making and judicious choice. Flash fiction can be read between subway stops, in stolen moments when the boss isn't looking, and by those who are tired and have no time for a longer short story. Why? Read one of the 100 featured and see for yourself. This will only take a minute.

Bruce Meyer

DIANA S. ADAMS

The Mirror

He arrived without warning, just past noon. *What would you like to talk about first?* he asked, looking past me through the window into the gated backyard garden. I needed to breathe deep a few times before I could speak. I poured us each a glass of red wine; we sat at the kitchen table. *You used to love working in that little yard,* he said, *even though nothing could ever grow in it, maybe that was the first sign that we* … His voice was a low whisper and raspy. I wasn't ready to talk about the past. I changed the subject. *How was Egypt?* He took a sip of wine. *It was fine, Egypt will always be … you know, my place. But I am there too often now, even in my dreams. You hated it.* I couldn't look at his eyes which were flat-black, and depthless. *Here, I brought you something.* He pulled out a package wrapped in gold tissue from his pants pocket and unwrapped it. It was a small hand-held gilt mirror. I wanted to touch his smooth hand, but he pulled it back quickly, with a reprimand in his eyes. *Just look into this whenever you think you miss me. I'll try to make myself available.* I didn't know what to say. I'm still not comfortable with the dead. And I wasn't sure I ever wanted to see him again.

Parlour

There's a room in your head, but the doorknob is hidden. You like it this way, a private space without noise or people. You tidy it daily, keep the lines neat, sprinkle water over the ferns and rearrange the furniture. The colours you chose are lime-white, mouse-back and fern slipper satin. But there is a hint of confusion in the air because you have arrived so late. And the room keeps growing larger. How many right angles can you see? How many wrong?

There is a rustling behind the curtains. You strain to see what it could be. All your dead relatives come out dragging tables and chairs with them. They sit down, start talking, play gin rummy and drink wine out of plastic tumblers, just as they always did on family vacations. Your ex-husband Thom is there too, the earlier version of himself, wearing the golf shirt you bought him before everything went wrong. He looks at you and winks. First, you feel excited, but then you weaken with the sadness of missing him as he was then, and the others.

You crouch behind the floral sofa. But your grandmother has just seen you, and now calls you over. She says you look grey and should lie down. Eat a cheese and cucumber sandwich, she says. Then your uncle Phil, your father and the sister Rebecca who died when she was ten all wave you over to sit with them. You can't hear what they are saying, all their words are pooling together. It's all too much, you're dizzy and you don't know how to deal with the dead. They don't look dead at all; their eyes are clear, hair shiny, and their skin is plump and pink.

You would love to see your sister again, and there is something you really need to tell Thom. Somehow you know you can't. Rubbing your pregnant belly you feel the kick of response. In a few weeks, your baby will enter this world. A world that even the dead don't want to leave. Turning your back on everyone's furious entreaties, you close your eyes, direct your mind to your appointment today and watch them drift away.

***Diana S. Adams** is an Edmonton, Alberta-based writer of poetry and fiction. Her latest book of poetry* Imported Poems *is published by BlazeVOX Books.*

BERT ALMON

Book of Condolences

After his father died, Betty's older son found out who she was and where she lived. She was very happy but a little afraid at their first meeting. She had recovered from alcoholism, but her lost family was untraceable, although she had set her parents and sister looking while she was in a series of rehabs. Her parents blamed themselves for her broken family: she started drinking from their liquor cabinet before she became a teenager. But it was her duty to make amends to them, the ninth step. Her son brought the bad news: his little brother died years ago. She made a heap of herself in the nearest chair, her teeth chattering. Finally, he brought out the black leatherette Book of Condolences from the funeral, with the dead son's photo at the front and a dried flower between two pages. He left it with her after their afternoon of tears and broken threads of memory. That night, she looked at the list of mourners and their consoling comments, hoping to learn a little about the dead boy's years without a mother. Her parents and sister were at the top of the list.

Bert Almon *has published ten collections of poems and won two Writers' Guild of Alberta awards. He taught creative writing at the University of Alberta for forty years.*

KRISTIN ANDRYCHUK

The Dandelion Bed

I need a magician tonight to take her home. This creature's skin hangs in folds like those hairless Chinese dogs. She is no puppy in a wrinkled hide, but brittle bones in an old skin.

Though I clothe her in a long flannel nightgown, sweater, flannelette sheets, three wool blankets and a thick comforter, I can't make her warm. Her knobbed feet are wrapped in the afghan and still she shivers.

Come magician, use your skill. Take her where she can garden for hours. Her hoe is deadly to dandelion, quack grass and plantain, but spares tomatoes, peppers, cabbage and corn.

Take her to a July day, 1944. Her two little girls, ill with measles, lie in a darkened room. Just one splinter of sun at the edge of the drawn blind. When she enters, the children are hot and whining, tired of paper, scissors and dolls. She covers the bed with newspapers, and before they can guess what she's going to do, dumps a whole bushel of dandelions on their bed and disappears.

Strange about those dandelions, how bright in that dark room. The girls make chains and crowns. Sniff their stained hands and cover each other in dandelion jewels. Bored with this they make cats and lions. It rains dandelions until the bed sprouts and a herd of petalled animals settle on the children's feet, rampage up and down their legs, and jump from lap to lap.

Ah, Mother, you are the magician, always were.

Holding It All

The floorboards creak, *Gone, gone, gone*. And I think of my brother who spent forty-four years here moving from room to room in his wheelchair. He told me about listening to the first Sputnik on his short-wave radio. He'd identified its evenly spaced *Dah, dah, dah*. Had a verification card from the Soviet Union. He said the listening took him beyond Earth. In this empty house, he whispers, "Go, go, go." He never begrudged me my going, my husband and children.

My sister and her sons left this morning with their load of family things. We cleaned from attic to cellar for the new owners. No point in keeping the house now, Mother lives with me.

We sent loads to the dump and the church rummage sale. Our voices echoed back and forth as we exclaimed over baby boots and old photographs on back closet-shelves. My sister called to me from my old room—yet another find, doll clothes we'd made with big uneven stitches when we were too young to safely use the sewing machine. We laughed at our excitement, our too-loud voices. She said, "It's like the first time we saw the place." And I remembered, we ran from room to room and, as the floors creaked, our brother said it was the dead owner walking.

I'm alone now. I think of Mother living here after my brother's death. She told me that, as night came on, she could feel her ghosts gathering. She liked to get in the house, get all the lights on. That's what I should do now. The big trailer is loaded. I even picked a bushel of pears. Such a bumper crop, the tree's branches touch the ground.

A five-hour drive, he should be here soon. I'm lucky to have a husband. He'll hook up the trailer, and we can go home tomorrow.

All the work is done. Yesterday I stroked the worn places on the big chair where a succession of cats slept. Tiger, Sarah, Ringtail, Muggins, Togo, Pinti, Boxcar: forty-four years of sleeping cats. Carrying the chair to the trailer, we caught it on the doorframe. A cloud of dust and hair rose as the fabric tore.

I cleared off the burled-walnut buffet: a stub from Mother's pension cheque, two condolence cards she'd saved, a small brass dog and a lace doily. Bared, it morphed into another piece of shabby furniture.

My voice bounces through empty rooms, nothing to catch it, not even memories. The house is clammy though a hot, August night. Open the door. Air it out. In the dark, branches rub porch screens. A cloudy night, a few stars glint through, light from suns dead a million years. An empty house between me and all that space.

I spread the pad mattress on linoleum patterned with marks from my brother's wheelchair. Make up the bed and smooth the quilt.

The traffic must be heavy. Come soon. I need you. Please hold me.

What Is Left

On a snowless January day with a grey sky, brown grass and dead hothouse flowers, I stand in the cemetery and look across the road at Mother's old house. Sold two years ago, do the new owners call it the Old Stanbury Place? Do their children scare each other with stories of dead Stanburys buried in the graveyard across the road?

Mother lived here forty-five years, but three cemetery plots are all we own of Ridgeway now. Long ago my sister and I sat on our catalpa's wide branches and watched the funerals. We listened to *The Last Post* and for a while after held military funerals for birds and mice our cats carried home.

I look at what is left of our catalpa. The tree, a giant trunk surrounded by downed branches, has been brutally pruned to make room for mock colonial porches and lighted gate posts. Will there be any white blossoms tinged with mauve and fan leaves next summer? The aging white house is exposed now, yet lost under plastic siding. For so many years that house was sheltered by overgrown lilac and orange blossom and towered over by the catalpa, its branches reaching almost to the front door.

I touch the cold black granite. Trace their names, Mother's now added to the rest. They don't belong here. Should be in the house across the road.

A door slams. A child laughs. I look up. Two little kids in pink and purple snowsuits are climbing on the downed branches. Now, they're riding them like horses. I want to yell, "Get out of my yard." I don't, of course.

Someday they will stand where I am. But for now, it is their time, their turn. Wish them well and walk away.

Tail-Fins and Chartreuse Houses

They're going to Kansas City to visit her dad's long-lost cousin. When Kate was little, she loved the *Oz* books, and that's as close to Kansas as she's been. Now she prefers Zane Grey. She used to like dog and horse stories too, but in 1951, she's growing up and so is everything else.

Even cars are getting bigger. Old cars look all squished up like squat old people. New cars are bright, not grey, black and navy blue, colours old ladies wear to church. Her father's car is dark red, but their neighbour's car is yellow with big fins and a silver horse on the hood.

Even the roads are new: the Queen Elizabeth Way, the New York State Thruway and, as they speed along, Cliffville, the pretend town of their childhood, comes to life—all the brightly coloured cars and trucks, like their toy ones. But Kate and Diane are too grownup for Cliffville now. Fifteen-year-old Diane has started ballet lessons, and all she wants to do is dance. A dancing school opened in the spring, a first for their small town.

Kate feels sorry for old things, barns, especially with sagging roofs. New houses are green, mauve, blue or multi-coloured angel stone. Old houses look like sad faces—pointed porch roofs are noses and the two windows above are eyes. The verandas become mouths. When the blinds are down, the old houses have gone to sleep. New houses have picture windows and jungly-flowered drapes.

She feels sorry for their old grey house with stains underneath its windows as if it's been crying. She wants a new house with all new things. She thinks her house will be mauve or maybe even chartreuse, this year's new colour.

So hot on this highway going to Kansas City. All the car windows are open. Her brother Chuck, who needs fresh air, rides upfront with their dad. She, her mother and Diane are crowded into the back. She sticks her head out the window. The wind blows her hair straight back. She laughs. Diane scowls and ties her kerchief tighter.

Everywhere she looks they're building something. All the orange and yellow machinery digging. Driving through construction zones, Kate and Diane sing, *Detour, detour, muddy road ahead*. The new Ford bounces along the gravel.

They eat at truck stops. Kate likes listening to the drivers talk, likes how they joke and always have money for the jukebox. Her brother chooses *A Room Full of Roses.* She puts the nickel in the slot.

Maybe someday she'll be a truck driver. Diane'll be a dancer, and Chuck'll be a writer. He graduated from the Cerebral Palsy School. He's already finished a detective story. In the Forties when the cars were as grey as the houses and Kate was little, she would've been just pretending. But the summer of 1951, riding in a big-finned Ford, she passes a chartreuse house and everything is possible.

On the Road

Our daughter drives, her father adjusts the radio, and I, nursing my arthritic back, am ensconced in pillows on the back seat. I gave up driving many years ago at sixty-five. "New evidence links the increased pollution in the Athabaska River to oil sands development." He turns off the news and puts on a CD. On the road again with Willie Nelson, the pale-green arch carries us over the St. Lawrence. Did the engineer who planned this bridge see the beauty in his design? Yes, there can be beauty in what people make—the great span of this bridge and on the island below, that white cabin, that red canoe. We aren't only Earth's destroyers, polluters. When I was fourteen, with just a learner's permit, legal in those days, the Peace Bridge—Fort Erie to Buffalo, marked a trip's beginning. My first time on the New York Thruway and Dad let me drive. We left at dawn—the fields misty-green, the highway a grey strip. I pushed the old Ford up to sixty and could've driven forever. And when would I ever be old enough to be on my own to see everything? Longing made my throat ache, the whole ball of the world unrolling before us. I am plenty old on this fall day when rain smears green, red, and yellow leaves to a kindergarten painting. Rain-water lying in fresh-turned furrows brings me to "wee sleekit, cowrin, tim'rous beastie" and the white-furred belly of the mouse I removed from the trap this morning. A small death in my small life. Nothing matters and everything matters. Give me one more family road trip, one more misty morning with the metronome of windshield wipers marking our passage on I-81 heading south.

Early Morning Blues

I'm wide awake again, the pillow is hard, the blankets heavy. A long wait till morning.

When will the dreams stop? I was on the couch with our grandson, reading to him *The Lion, the Witch and the Wardrobe,* when Mother appeared. She had on the old beat-up running shoes she wore for weeding. She started telling him a story: "We lived in a tent while fixing up the old cabin and canoed across the lake to get supplies ..."

I woke up with a start knowing my mother died over twenty years go and that little boy is now a teenager. Will he drop out of school? I know he's drinking and smoking. Is it drugs too? He was such a bright little boy, but so vulnerable. Is he scared? That's the worst. When he used to stay overnight, I'd say to him as I tucked him in, "Did you have a good day?" Who did I think I was to believe I could fix things? The weather forecast said snow. He drives too fast. What if there's black ice?

Get out of bed. Go downstairs. Make coffee.

As I stir milk into my coffee, I think of Mother, when she couldn't sleep, doing the same. So many years alone with her ghosts in that old house.

Snow at dawn falls softly, covering brown November. A granddaughter's drawing on the fridge door smiles at me, and I stir up a cake for her mother's, my daughter's forty-sixth birthday.

Kant said time is a category of the human mind. All of this is one moment in eternity. Does that make it less scary? Not really. But once a person dies, they are no longer old. She is alive in me—my mother, the courageous child, the young woman, and the old one. Time is erased, and all is present tense—or past. Doesn't matter now.

I let the cat out the back door. The flurries feel good against my face. One streak of light in the east. Don't turn away. A new categorical imperative. See it. Feel it.

Place and family are major influences in the stories ***Kristin Andrychuk*** *tells through her poetry, short stories and novels. She has four published novels.*

MATTHEW CHARLES BARRON

His Prices

Tilson talked furniture the way other East Van shopkeepers sold it. His showroom was a chatty concatenation of the rarest tables, the most discontinuous sofas, odds and sods for sale or possibly storage, an ambiguity that boggled the tip-toeing few who, seeking a path to purchase, snailed between wobbly stacks of trundles, lampstands, wardrobes. Many chimed right back out the door.

Living directly upstairs, Talia owed much of her adulthood to the shop below. Dizzy, headachy most nights after another day of underreported overwork, she bought a Shaker downstairs, a Morris chair, so many furnishings that Tilson joked about sinking an elevator up to her bachelor. When she tired of Bergère—his warehouse, he said, had more Wishbones than a holiday bird—she could return her Wingback down the lift and he'd toss in this green alien floor lamp. A curio no competitor could offer.

If you can't afford the sticker shock, consider this a rehearsal for the sale, he said—no money down. Or wait a week for him to liquidate another estate auction. A sale is like the future, he always said, dragging his smoke through another coughing fit: it needs plenty of room to arrange itself in. For this reason, he stayed open 52-7, even on holidays. Sometimes Talia wondered if Tilson, silvered enough to be her father, had a walkup somewhere, or squeezed his winks behind the inventory.

More and more often after work, he'd catch her up on the backstairs, leaving her guilt-ridden about leaning away from another how-are-you.

He should let her go, he said. He wasn't imposing any more Hepplewhite on her, or American Empire. The only true empire is family, always imposing, always stifling, always criticizing.

You just remind me of someone, he mumbled back up the stairwell, as if worried she could accuse him of other designs.

Having had a lung complaint scoped too late, Tilson died the following year with an unexpectedness that Talia realized should have been expected. Somehow, her friend, looking fifty on a sunny day, was a posthumous eighty. Soon, a familiarly aged woman came from away to dissolve the shop.

Let me guess, she said. Tilson had never mentioned his older sister.

Deborah studied as if specking the linoleum. She'd already exchanged more words with Talia than she had with her own brother in 30 some odd years. They lived on opposing coasts, and it was all over something that was said on the 17th of May.

Driving soft bargains is hard for some, she said. But it was important Tilly's inventory be sold to neighbours, not liquidators, and over the following weeks Deborah unburdened the stock, seeming to pride herself on leaving it Tilson-cluttered.

If she had never cared for her brother's prices, she said, some time ago she had begun, unfortunately, to exact her own.

***Matthew Charles Barron** is a Vancouver-based fiction and communications writer. He holds an MA and has attended literary workshops at the Banff Centre and other institutions.*

ROSANNA MICELOTTA BATTIGELLI

The Sense of It All . . .

She stares at me sometimes from behind her front window. I see the slight ripple of the silk curtain. I wait for her hands to appear and nudge it aside, but she doesn't always want to be seen.

I slowly drive by her house today and decide to stop. She's tending the patch of poppies in her side yard. I roll down my window but she doesn't notice me.

She gives an irritated groan as she slowly unbends, rubbing her arthritic knees. She looks up into the cherry tree that's ripe with berries before shifting her gaze to the ground, the red-tinged pits studding the grass and cement walkway. She mumbles, "Those damn birds, making such a mess, because I don't have enough work to do around here!" And then she gives a dismissive wave. "I suppose they have to eat, too . . ."

She shuffles to the back, where her bean and basil plants await their daily watering. Then she sets down her watering can and plods up the ramp to the side door and enters. Moments later, I see her behind the curtain. This time her hands appear, as my hands tremble slightly at the wheel. I feel a sting behind my eyelids as my gaze shifts to the SOLD sign in the front yard, and I wonder who will be keeping a garden now. Next to the sign, the peonies are just about to bloom. I can almost smell their candy-sweet fragrance. My gaze shifts back to the window.

My mother's hands are gone.

Soon, the curtains will probably be gone, too.

I stare at the silk flowers on the passenger seat. My throat constricts as I head to the cemetery, leaving the chirping birds to their cherry feast.

Rosanna Micelotta Battigelli *is the award-winning author of* La Brigantessa, Pigeon Soup & Other Stories, *five Harlequin romances, and two children's books. www.rosannabattigelli.com*

DESSA BAYROCK

The Patron Saint of Butchers is also the Patron Saint of Surgeons and Abortions

Tell me the story about the chef who cuts off his own leg and eats it, Darcy says, and I don't know what she's talking about, which means she wants me to make it up. *Paired well with a nice Chianti*, I say, and she laughs. *You know nothing about wine*, she says. And, for a while, I think that's the end of it.

Tell me about the boy born without knees? she asks, the two of us bundled in our parkas and nudging up against each other like Michelin Men. I tell her: *Nobody pegged him for a long-jump champion, but here we are.* She snorts. The landscape whizzes by outside the window but then it slows, and stops, and it's Darcy's stop. *See you later, Michelin Man, love of my life*, and she grins before the door shuts her out and she becomes part of the landscape blurring by, just like everything.

What about the woman who drowned her children? she asks, her hands turning to the last plate in the sink. I can hardly hear her over the running water. I hesitate. *She faked their deaths,* I say. *Sure*, Darcy snorts, and slams the plate on the rest of the stack and leaves the kitchen.

That night, long after she's asleep, I curl myself around her. *He only cooked his leg because he didn't have anything left to feed his family*, I whisper. *And the patron saint of butchers took pity on him, and traded the leg out for a leg of lamb, and let him forget how the knife plunged into his body like a terrible dream.*

But what did the knife dream about? she asks, and I see that her eyes have been open all along. But for this, like everything, I have no answer.

Dessa Bayrock *is a PhD Candidate living on unceded Algonquin territory. You can find her, or at least more about her, at dessabayrock.com.*

WADE CRAVATH BELL

The Sturgeon

There was a creek that flowed into the North Saskatchewan after the river curved northward and left Edmonton for Fort Saskatchewan, then a village unaware of its future as a sprawling suburb of cracking towers and metallurgical refineries.

Nostalgic at eighty, the Old Man remembers going to that creek with his parents. They took a streetcar to the end of the line and walked the rest of the way. This was in 1946. His father had served in the Royal Canadian Air Force. He had not been home for long.

The Old Man was four or five. He held his mother's hand but not his father's. He didn't know his father well. He had no evidence that he could trust him.

It seemed like a long walk. The air was clean. The massive industrialization of the area later changed that.

There may have been a road to the creek. If there was, it wouldn't have made a difference because they didn't have a car.

They walked down the bluff on a trail bordered by saskatoon bushes. They picked some saskatoons. When they got to the creek, they ate them with their lunch. His lunch was a Velveeta cheese sandwich. It was what he asked for every day.

There was a log across the creek. He walked across the log and was scared but did it and felt good when he got to the other side. He thought the stream was wide. It probably wasn't. The fish lying motionless in it seemed huge.

His father said the fish was a sturgeon. Stupidly, or maybe too shyly, he asked his father what a sturgeon was. His father pointed to the fish. He said that was what a sturgeon was. He remembers the remark as an early lesson in ichthyology and belittling adult logic.

The fish was mesmerizing. It stayed in a pool in the creek for a long time. He thought it was dead before he saw the gills moving. They moved like a dog slowly panting. Was it sick? he wondered. It was exciting when it finally left the pool. Swimming away, it was almost as wide as the creek.

They sat on a faded red blanket on the sandy soil at the river's edge. There was enough current in the wide river to make the water gently lap the shore. The saskatoons were slightly sour.

When it came time to leave, he was tired and probably cranky but when his father put him on his shoulders and carried him back across the log then all the way up to the streetcar stop, he was happy.

That year his father built a house for them on the South Side, on 79th Avenue. Like that house, the creek doesn't exist anymore.

By the Bar Sporting

San Juan de la Cruz and Thomas de Quincy: is it only because I read them together, pages of one, pages of the other, that I see resemblances? Over the morning's second *café con leche* and croissant with butter and strawberry jam, I get that both, in their way, were addicts. Via their given ecstasy—their Molly—both reached for existential heights and both bore witness to failure's agony.

Don't we all have withdrawal pain? Or is it only we depressives with our wonky, overactive subgenual cingulates?

There is a deal of pain to get through. Hour by hour, minute by minute, the day passes. Unlike de Q, opium as opium is not my problem. It's not an opioid I want tonight, that I will want in the morning.

But I am addicted. And a fool because of it. Juan's bane and mine: beautiful earthly love. The beloved's sweet embracing arms. Gurgling brooks, laughing wine, dark nights brightened as only romance can brighten them. Those sorts of things.

This is me. Here again at three a.m. under the poplars in the plaza by the Bar Sporting de Gracia (Gracia: Barrio of Grace) in Barcelona, Spain. I am watching lovers sway to a raspy, almost unheard, saxophone. Leaves shiver in a whisper of wind. She is late but she arrives.

She occupied my mind like thunder the sky. The silence that followed was a wound filled with her. As Juan's cell silently overflowed with Santa Teresa de Avila, her body in the rounded stones of the walls of his medieval prison. In the dark, memories shine like midday light.

Two centuries ago in this year, 2021, Thomas de Q of London knew loneliness. He had no one to turn to. Took opium, heard voices, felt others gathering around him to make him safe. San Juan de la Cruz, Saint John of the Cross, prisoner in a monastery at Toledo four hundred and eighty years ago, also knew what a deadly partner for the dance loneliness was.

Tomorrow, Easter Monday, I will wake up. I will wake up. I will wake up, I promise. The coffee will be fine, the croissants perfect, and I, head bent, will give thanks to the spiritual opulence of the sacred day and the honesty of promises made so long ago.

Then I will wake her and we will dance.

Note: Molly is a street name for the psychoactive drug MDMA.

Wade Bell *lives in Calgary. He has also lived in Edmonton, Ottawa and Barcelona, Spain. Guernica Editions has published three books of his stories.*

JOHN BLAIR

Morder

She's gone and it's all my fault.

Loneliness is just a word, but it sure can choke you.

A few steps out the door and my sore eyes are treated to the neighbours' well-tended lawns. I take a few deep breaths and begin my after-dinner stroll.

Having covered two blocks, I take the narrow path leading to the dog park.

"Alex!"

I turn around and smile at Tom.

"Hey there."

His Labrador bares its teeth and growls at me.

"What's eating Morder today?"

I'm making sure to keep a good distance from them.

"Strange," Tom says. "He's like that with people he doesn't know. But he knows you."

"How is everything?"

"Ah, don't ask. This damn stay-at-home bullshit. I'm taking the dog out early tonight to get away from Susan—and save my sanity."

"I guess we're all getting on each other's nerves these days."

The truth of what I've just said tightens my throat.

Tom figures I want to hear his whole story which I don't.

"She's got this new recipe for penne. I ask her to pass the pepper, and she starts screaming. 'You don't need to add anything to it. It's a perfect dish as is.' I tell you, sometimes I dream about walking out on her and never coming back."

Morder barks at me and Tom gives him a shut-up scowl.

"Listen," I say, "when the temperature gets too hot, we have to bring it down, right?"

"Say what?"

"Next time Susan starts shouting, speak softly to her. Say you're sorry. Ask her how you can help."

Now I'm wondering why I didn't take my own advice. It would certainly have prevented the problems I see ahead for me.

"I never thought about that."

Tom pats me on the shoulder.

"Thanks, buddy. Say hello to Dianne for me when you get home."

"Sure."

But I know I won't.

Once I get home, I'll have to untie the scarf from around her neck.

John Blair *is a high school English teacher from Toronto. His young adult novel,* Hockey Camp Summer, *is available from Amazon.*

DIANE BRACUK

Pert Posterior

You hate yourself when you're like this.

Obsessively clicking onto the snarky celebrity website which has a post of the two of you—*the loved up pop star couple!*—frolicking in the Malibu surf, you "*flashing a pert posterior in a skimpy thong bikini!*" Shameless clickbait. Over a thousand comments, more coming in. Even though you've assured your therapist that you'll quit visiting this site for the sake of your mental health, you've read almost all of them.

The negative comments, like the one you just read, you're supposed to visualize flowing out of your head like water. But only the positive ones (and there are many, far more than the mean ones, with your fans praising you for being such a good role model for promoting body positivity, your commendable acceptance of your cellulite and weight gain) flow out. The mean ones stick like broken Lego bits in your aching brain, non-biodegradable. *Stump legs. Packing on the pudge. Maybe she's OK with embracing her cellulite, but it looks like he isn't.*

What signs did you miss, you wonder, clicking back onto the verboten post and zooming in. Look at him, relaxed and smiling in baggy surfer shorts guys get to wear, and look at you, back contorted in a painful looking twist to display your not-so-pert posterior at the most flattering angle for the paparazzi lurking on the beach. All staged, having to create the illusion that it was completely spontaneous. Exposure, your publicist said, before you both took an extended break to recharge after your exhausting world tour.

Does a man ever look more attractive than when he's about to end things with you? His Byronic curls—the ones tween girls swoon over—graze his shirt collar, his long lanky legs stretch out like muscular tent poles. You planned this break for so long, the two of you alone at last, out of the public eye—long conversations, cooking, making love slowly—that it took you a while to register what he was saying.

No, not taking a break. Breaking. Up. With you.

At your most recent session, your therapist expressed concern that you were sinking into a self-loathing depressive state.

"The negative comments will poison you," she said.

"I know, but I've always been super self-critical ..."

"He didn't break up with you because you gained weight. This was the first romantic relationship for both of you. You still have his friendship."

"I know."

"I want you to tell me one nice thing someone said about you lately."

"Some troll called Dickepedia said that he'd still stick it in my wicket."

Your therapist frowns.

"I thought it was funny," you say. Then start crying.

Your phone looks strangely bloated, like a pregnant black beetle, new comments swelling inside like larvae, ready to burst into a swarm of buzzing negative nits. And you, the patron saint of cellulite, the role model so many young girls look up to.

One last time you tell yourself, clicking in. The very last.

***Diane Bracuk** is the author of* Middle-Aged Boys & Girls, *published by Guernica Editions, which was nominated for The Ontario Library Association's 2017 Evergreen Award.*

LARRY BROWN

Flintstones

Kayla says she won't be, not anyone's. Worse, she won't be my girlfriend either. All those apologies, she says, with that whispering Irish accent, an accent I hear in my dreams though in my dreams it's not always Irish, and not always Kayla speaking it.

We're in the school library, I'm hauling around books on the Industrial Revolution, Kayla's perfume reminds me of cherries. Apologies? I say, but with some hush to my voice. Nobody has to be sorry, I say, the hush lost. Kayla moves along the aisle, away from me, head bent, reading book spines. Or pretending to. I can't tell.

I'm fifteen, I'm no thesaurus, I know what I feel, only not in words.

Yet we hold hands while we sit a cushion apart on the blue couch in my parents' basement and watch TV. And together we unravel, probably mangle, what they say on the French station, then we search the channels for a movie, a black and white one if we're lucky, with hats and a big story. We drink chocolate milk from Flintstones glasses. Between us, we split a Milky Way bar.

Matty, what is this pandemonium we're watching? Kayla likes to say.

No one else does that, speaks my name and makes it a richer thing than it is.

Today, after an hour of sampling our way up and down the channels, I click the remote and the screen goes blank. It is raining outside, the basement dim, our milk glasses empty. This is the part where, usually, with barely a word and regardless of the weather, Kayla stands,

Kayla leaves, as if needing to be somewhere else right away. The part where, usually, I wait to see her legs in their black tights walk by the basement window so I can try to will them to stop and bring her, bring that accent, back to the blue couch.

Today, Kayla doesn't get up. As she did yesterday, she says, Can we stay here for now, Matty? Yesterday, she squeezed my hand and my leg shook.

But my question today is this: Why am I about to say something I know I'll have to apologize for?

HC

The first of September arrived. My father washed his face then opened the hall closet door and reached up and took it down, the soft wool cap. In its place he put the box holding his straw fedora. The summer fedora with the smudged dents where he always pinched to pick up or adjust the hat. It's that time, I heard him say.

On the first of October he exchanged his sleeveless undershirts—undershirts that provided a bridge from Labour Day to the start of October—for undershirts with sleeves. Short sleeves. Pocket? No. V-neck? Never. Squirrels gathered nuts while my father layers clothes, winter, apparently, icing up the horizon.

For TV watching in the cooler months he added a blanket. Each night, sleep drew him down into the chair, the TV blaring. An hour, maybe two, later he drifted back to the surface and, blinking, pieced the clues together, figuring out where he was. And why. Eventually he got up, spread the newspaper across the kitchen table, his bleary eyes clearing as they moseyed along and massaged meaning from the squiggles on the page. He always read standing up, hands flat-palming the table. Then he would snack. Cereal, a banana, and chocolate. Always some chocolate.

After my mother died, I moved back to live with him and help out. Often we passed in the hall at five a.m., my father finally going to bed and me rising for work. Neither of us ever spoke at these meetings. Instead, we exchanged a sort of hello-but-I'm-on-my-way-elsewhere expression.

One weekend afternoon I was gathering clothes for a wash and came upon my father standing at the kitchen table in his newspaper-reading pose. But in place of the newspaper was a calendar, the free one that came in the local paper before Christmas.

The winning cover art prize that year went to an eight-year-old for her drawing of the moon and sun with long arms and dancing legs, while a pair of dogs, one yellow and one blue, deposited empty dog food cans into a recycling bin.

My father was counting and then writing something on the calendar, the same thing over and over. HC. He had gotten all the way until December. Next December.

Hair cut, he said when I asked. Every three weeks, you see, keeps it manageable.

But, he said to me, then pointed the pen at Christmas and New Year's on the calendar. Both were on a Tuesday. He made a sound. In eleven months his haircut-every-three-weeks schedule would be in peril.

I recognized and, more than I liked, understood the expression on his face.

***Larry Brown** lives in Brantford, Ontario. His story collection* Talk *was published by Oberon Press, and his story 'Triangle' appeared in* Best Small Fictions 2017.

MICHAEL E. CASTEELS

Fleas

The day begins bleakly. A red carnival tent squats on a grey landscape. A hung-over clown perches on the edge of his cot, horking a ball of phlegm into an empty tin can. Yesterday's face paint is worn thin on his cheeks, his purple wig pulled back, revealing a receding hairline. He stands, approaches a mirror, attempts a smile, but it falters into a grimace. He scans the ground for his red nose thinking it rolled off in the middle of the night. He searches under his pillow, then checks beneath the cot. He looks across the floor and remembers that meatball song from his childhood. Where had his poor nose rolled off to? Out the door? Into the world at large? His stomach growls, a reminder that he hasn't eaten since yesterday's breakfast, and that, only a bowl of stale, dry cereal, his milk having gone lumpy the day before. He pats his pockets, pulls out a bouquet of silk flowers, a rubber chicken, and a pack of cigarettes. He places one between his lips, fishes around his pockets and retrieves a miniature pistol. He points it at his chin, and pulls the trigger. A small flame dances on the tip of the barrel. He lights his smoke, and sits back down savouring his first taste of the day. Next will be some instant coffee, then he'll track down that nose. Maybe he'd left it with the acrobats or lost it in a game of poker with the lion tamer. He racks his brain but comes up with nothing but an empty bottle, overly large shoes, a hoop of fire, and the little car that everyday seems harder to fit into. The car was shrinking. Hell, the whole circus was shrinking. He knows eventually they'll all be fleas, suspended over a fine wire of disbelief. He exhales and coughs fitfully. Then he horks again, with perfect aim, into the can with a crisp ding.

Walking the Old Dog

My dog had lost a toe. I don't know when or how it happened. I was drying him off after a rainy walk when I noticed a gap in his left hind paw. He didn't seem bothered by the loss, he wasn't in any pain that I could see. Still, I thought it best to take him to the vet.

"I wouldn't worry too much," the vet said. "He's not a young dog anymore. Keep feeding him well and give him some love. He'll be fine."

But the next day I noticed another toe was gone, and the day after that too. I called the clinic, but the vet just said, "It's part of the aging process, it happens to us all."

My dog was stiff, and our walks, while getting shorter, took much longer. I let him linger on every good smell he could find.

One morning his tail had vanished. I searched the entire house, but to no avail. Now it was little stub that vibrated when he got excited.

Later, I called him for his walk but he didn't come. I found him curled on his bed, asleep and dreaming. His ears were gone, he couldn't hear a thing. I woke him with a soft pat, and clipped on his leash. Slowly he got to his feet and shuffled along.

By the time we got home he'd lost a hind leg. But he still seemed his happy, old self. I gave him a treat and he made his way back to bed.

It was happening too fast. One day he was fine, and a week later he'd nearly disappeared. That evening I looked in on him, and there was only his head smiling up at me. He licked my hands when I picked him up and I was reminded of him as a puppy, when he'd get tired on our long walks. He'd stop, and I'd have to carry him. Like his head now, he fit perfectly in the crook of my arm.

The next day I woke up, and his head was gone. Only his collar remained. I clipped on his leash and took him out for a walk. It was a bright morning, early spring. I stopped to let him linger at all the good smells along the way.

Michael e. Casteels *is the workhorse behind Puddles of Sky Press. His most recent book of poetry is the minimalist, meta-western* The Man with the Spider Scar.

KIM CONKLIN

Thursday Girls

They come every Thursday, exactly at eleven-thirty. They're early because they're over eighty and rise well before the sun, and because they want to make sure they arrive before the quiche sells out.

I'd save them the quiche, but I don't need to. They're never late.

They have nothing in common. One's a prim retired secretary, married to a retired policeman. Another buried three husbands: a doctor, a lawyer and a judge. The third was a hairdresser and a divorcée from the day she opened her own shop, and the fourth is a farm wife, mother of six, and grandmother of twenty. I've been waiting on them for two decades, since the diner became a vegetarian tearoom.

That was B.B.—before bunions.

They were never friends, but when they bumped into each other —each surviving a ten-car pile-up on Route 4 without a scratch—they saw the sign. No red hats for them. They don't seek attention: they give it. Comfort, confidence, whatever's needed, wherever, an emotional Meals-on-Wheels available everywhere, but with weekly board meetings. They used to bring photos in plastic sleeves, now they bring cell phones and boundless energy.

This wise constellation radiates light over the dining room. "Look how big!" they coo to the infants. "You can do it," they say to drained young mothers, and "You are beautiful" to chubby teenagers and "Love will come" to lonely young working girls.

They prop up forty-something women whose lives have ceased to be their own. They nod knowingly while listening to tales of days lost to care and feeding and ego-building and accepting faults and covering failures and ignoring mistakes—and being ignored.

The ladies know most things will not turn out as planned. The children will not become star athletes or scientists, husbands will see wives as a pair of worn slippers, and these women, too, will cease to exist except in moments of domestic ritual, captured in snapshots, proof that happiness is possible, if only for a split second.

Thousands and thousands of snapshots have crossed this table, narrated, clung to, commented on and validated. What these four women understand, why others seek them out, is the tiny pictures never quite add up to a big one, but when you realize there is no big picture, small moments become enough, like waking up everyday with courage and, if possible, hope. I clear the plates and pour fresh tea. Then I pick up a camera and motion for a group shot.

"Move closer," I say, "and smile."

My bunions are swollen and sore, but Thursday lunch shift is better than Tylenol.

Kim Conklin *is a writer, filmmaker and podcaster. Kim's stories and films have appeared in journals, anthologies and film festivals. A novel is forthcoming (2022).*

JORDAN ELLIOTT

Meditations While Falling from a Medium-sized Building

I always thought that I'd go to Medieval Times. I thought I'd like to watch some sword-fighting, eat a big turkey leg, drink a mug of ale, which I'm sure is actually a plastic cup of some domestic light beer, but at least with some kind of knightly logo on it. Like a ballpark beer, right? With that condensation sweating down the sides of it? You know what I mean. It has to be plastic, I'm guessing, because you can't serve beer in real ale mugs or drinking horns at Medieval Times: too breakable, too much temptation for people who feel they've already overpaid for admission and a turkey leg to keep them, a sneaky souvenir, thinking that they're owed something more than the big show. I don't know. We're all selfish, deep down. But really, I think I wanted to go to Medieval Times because I've always been a coward and I'm curious about courage. I mean, I know that all the bravery there is fake: those lances that the knights use are definitely designed to break away at the faintest contact, I'm sure, and the armour is probably triple-padded or made from space-age polymers, there's too much insurance liability otherwise. And you have to think that the winners are predetermined at the afternoon meeting: "Okay Green Knight, you win the sword fight, and Red, it's been a while since you won the joust, so you win today." But even knowing all that, the appearance of bravery, even fake bravery, is something I just don't understand. I've always taken the easy way out, I always run away. When armies shoot their own retreating soldiers, that's where I'd be, in the pile of that first wave of quitters. But I always thought I'd go to Medieval Times at least once, just to watch, and eat a turkey leg, and drink a plastic cup of beer, so I'll just add it to my prodigious list of failures. And the closest one is all the way in Toronto anyways.

Jordan Elliott *(MFA, School of the Art Institute of Chicago; 2021 SAIC Writing Fellow) was born and raised in Alberta, and now lives in Virginia.*

Sara and Little Joe

Even an ocean away, I can imagine Sara's house. It is 6 p.m. and the porch lamp flickers orange. Through a window, I see her family eating dinner. Giuseppe presides over the table, cutting a fetina. Little Joe sits to his right, trying to pry the pit out of an apricot, and Lucia to his left, nibbling on a scrap of bread. Sara excuses herself. She skitters to the oven, a warm womb that radiates gold, and pulls out a loaf dusted with sunflower seeds.

Swatting the air with a mappina to dissipate yeasty-smoke, she overhears her husband say, "Joe, what you doing?"

"The stone won't come out."

"See these? They're tough hands."

Little Joe touches his own smooth knuckles. "Mine aren't like that, Papa."

"They will be. You just work hard."

Sara stretches knife through crackly crust, crossing into the soft and steaming. "Why don' you tell your daughter that, ah?" Giuseppe grabs a peach and carves out the pit. Little Joe squeezes his own apricot, confused as his papa bestows a slice of fruit to Lucia.

Giuseppe gives each child one bacioni e pizzicunedri, then kisses Sara's cheek. He's ready for a night of gambling with the men who were once his fellow bordanti. Little Joe waves, and once his papa has left, pouts at his mamma. Sara squawks the okay and he lunges to the television.

She's written meals are fine—I translate that into "buona" for our Mamma.

From the kitchen, Sara eyes Little Joe on the couch. He's astonished by Billy the Kid, gripping a cardboard pistol constructed from toilet paper rolls. Lucia plays with four uncooked rigatoni, a pasta family with doodles of eyes and mouths.

Sara places a plate of warm bread on the coffee table. "Joe, mangia." Lucia waits for her name to be called, but Sara walks away. "He's out again, leave me here."

Hearing this, Little Joe worries—why does his papa leave every night? And why does he always look tired, head heavy at dinner? Suddenly worried his father is gone, Little Joe screams "You're wrong!" at his mamma and pounds fist into the pasta family. They scatter and crack. Lucia cries. Sara whips her red slipper at Little Joe's feet but he dodges the shot. "Bring it back," she commands. Little Joe scuttles toward his mamma with the shoe, giggling while hunching to protect himself. Sara snatches it to smack her boy's arm, but with him squirming, only manages to swat his bum. As he scurries away, she glimpses the little boy that used to clutch her floral apron as they baked together.

Sara swaddles the crumby leftovers in a mappina and nestles them into breadbox. She watches Little Joe cheering for Billy's bullets, which dribble hot onto a wooden porch. She wonders when he will be home, heaving the flour bag out of the cupboard to bake her son more bread.

Antonia Facciponte *is a Toronto author. She received her Master's Degree in English from UofT. Her first book is titled* To Make a Bridge.

CYNTHIA FLOOD

At The Drugstore

Ahead of me stood a middle-aged woman, well-dressed, talking with the cashier as he rang up perfumes, bath oils and powders, throws of silky fabric, and dumped them into a plastic Christmas bag.

She'd soon travel to Brittany, he to Normandy, and neither happily.

"Family," she said. "Nothing worse."

"You got that right," in a flat tone, keying in prices.

"My son just phoned, he flew over there a few days ago. He's like *When you're here, Mum, don't be on your phone all the time!*" Pause, eyebrows up. "Of course, speaking for the grandparents! Doing their business."

"Classic," the cashier said. "Last summer, Mum came for a week. Seven days. I mean she *arrived.* Who invited her? A one-bedroom I have. She said, just before leaving, *I've never felt more unwelcome.*" A pause. "So. I'm like, *I'm forty-two. Stop trying to change me. I'm who I am, same as you.*"

The woman nodded. "Good. But this time I'm getting done with family first. Then I'll join my friends and have fun."

"Good strategy," he said. "Happy New Year!"

"Same to you."

He handed over her bag—then smiled towards me. I'd have loved more detail but lacked the nerve to ask, so just gave him my toothpaste.

Cynthia Flood *has published five books of short fiction, the most recent* What Can You Do *(2017). Her* Selected Stories *will appear in 2022 (Biblioasis).*

MARK FOSS

Mary Zimmerman from Wisconsin

At breakfast, although she's showing a loft in a few hours, Marie-Claire presses me for details. Who? How? When? And, above all, where? For Marie-Claire, it's all about location. Sometimes I answer a question with a question, and then watch her squeal with embarrassed laughter when she recognizes her own sales trick. Today, I play it straight, telling her the name uttered in my sleep belongs to a girl I pined over in grade school. My face is so transparent she knows I'm speaking the truth. I'm relieved she lets it drop. It's too ridiculous to admit I only knew the girl from ads for the American Seed Company in my comic books. While Joel Ballenger from Washington and William Hanlin from Missouri bragged about their sales, Mary Zimmerman's testimonial exuded a quiet, unassuming confidence: "It's an easy way to earn money and prizes." Although selling seeds was not easy at all, I did earn enough points for a chemistry set. On our second date in Old Montreal, I told Marie-Claire how a comic book ad had planted the seeds for my career. She smiled blankly, neither laughing nor grimacing at such a bald metaphor. It was a question of language, I thought, because her English was not great back then. She was more interested in the future of my research than its origins, joking I might one day discover a cure for cancer. For my part, I was seduced by accounts of her life in real estate. I wonder if Mary Zimmerman parlayed her early success into a sales career. Or maybe Mary, too, was inspired by the beakers and test tubes, the vials of dry chemicals, and all the iron filings in the chemistry set. Her research may also have started with great promise, and now she takes satisfaction from mentoring a new generation as I do. This girl was likely concocted in some

Manhattan boardroom to seduce impressionable kids like me. But it's never stopped me from dreaming. At the cocktail hour that opens the conference in Madison, Wisconsin, next month, in a ballroom with towering windows that overlook the city's most popular attractions, I will share my Mary Zimmerman story with another delegate. I will confess my marriage has lacked chemistry from the start. Her lips will curl in barely discernible amusement.

***Mark Foss** is the author of two novels, including* Molly O. *A third novel was shortlisted for the 2020 Guernica Prize. Visit him at www.markfoss.ca.*

LUCIA GAGLIESE

How-Do-You-Do?

If the executives think of George at all, they agree he's a fine fellow, a good elevator operator, reliable, pleasant. Most ask "How-do-you-do?" when they first see him, but they don't care about the response, which is always, "Very well, Sir, and you?" The executives only care that he hears their floor request and stops the elevator in perfect alignment before opening the door.

If they notice him at all, they put his age at about fifty, maybe a little older. They wonder what work he did before Otis installed the elevator. They guess correctly that it was manual labour, but none bothers to find out he spent twenty years making bricks deep in the Don River Valley, that he is proud of that work, excelled at it, but an injury forced him to find something easier.

If they chat with him, which occasionally they do, they are surprised he is well spoken and knowledgeable about current affairs, the Great War, and history. He is against prohibition and women's suffrage. He is keen on the new hockey league, although he's never played the sport himself.

If they have a proper conversation with him, but none of them ever will, they'll learn he's married and had two children, Stephen and Hilda. He will tell them Stephen died just after the war from tuberculosis and he doesn't hear much from Hilda. She wasn't the same after the home for unwed mothers, he'll explain. And if he's had a few drinks, he might even tell them he regrets ever sending her there, that he looks for a family resemblance in the face of every little boy he sees, that he resents his wife, Eliza, because it was her idea to send Hilda away. More likely, he'll just tell them Hilda has moved away, possibly back to England to her grandmother, and that Eliza is a salesgirl at Eaton's, in ladies' gloves.

If they befriend him, they'll discover George avoids going home most evenings. And they'll never see (because to meet her, so much else must happen first) the shadows of grief and worry in Eliza's eyes. They'll never hear her tell that George sits in the darkened kitchen at night, drinking bootleg whiskey and talking to photographs of his children. She'll never tell them that, during her streetcar rides to and from Eaton's, she rehearses what she'll say to George some day. They'd agree she must pick the right moment—when he's sober, when she doesn't have one of her headaches, when he isn't so far into himself that he isn't really there, when she can look at him without rage churning her gut.

They'll never know, see or hear any of this, those executives filing in and out of George's elevator, wearing their fancy suits and crisp fedoras, chatting up the office girls, making their floor requests, mumbling "How-do-you-do?" and not listening to the answer.

Lucia Gagliese's *stories have appeared or are forthcoming in* Best Canadian Stories, The New Quarterly, *and others. She is a professor at York University in Toronto.*

MARTY GERVAIS

Espoir, the Cow

Summer of 1749 on the French Settlement
on the South Shore of the Detroit River

It was the end of summer, and he didn't know what else to do. He spotted the cow struggling in the river, and quickly swam out to it, but turned to hear his wife's voice calling from the shoreline, as she made her way into the dark water to come and help. She had lifted up her skirt as if to take an operatic bow before wading knee-deep into the cold river, the panic in her voice obscured by the weary cow that bellowed and bellowed in the summer air until it had nothing more to say. As he eased his way toward the cow, he cursed himself for not bringing a rope, or something, anything, to lead it back to shore. Instead he floated with her, his only farm animal, other than a miserable hog that had accompanied him across the Atlantic. For now, he spoke to his cow in a soothing voice promising to grant her the moon and the sun and everything in between, and maybe he'd offer her a name. If she'd only just follow him back to the shore and scramble up to the pasture beyond. He didn't want to lose her. He'd only been here a few weeks. Minutes later, his wife joined the two, her skirts floated up around her like an unfurled map, and now the two led the way back for their cow. The three seemingly buoyant and carefree under a blue sky, but he never took his eyes off the cow as its big head bobbed up and down on the surface of the water. It was in that moment he noticed something of fear in his cow's luminous eyes. Or concern. Or worry. Or was it hope?

He whispered he'd baptize her *Espoir* if she reached the muddy beach, and soon she was there, free now of the river, her sagging girth drawn to the tall grass that gleamed in the morning sunlight.

***Marty Gervais** is a writer and photographer, Windsor's Poet Laureate Emeritus, and author of* The Hands, *published by Guernica Editions.*

BEN BERMAN GHAN

What?

Eyes closed. My breath makes noise. My fingers make noise. My own sounds are easy. They're inside. I do my best, in quiet rooms, and close company. I try, crooked, my left side reaching out, turning noise into words. Sometimes I can:

—Because like, you can't call it special needs, you know? Because like, you don't want to affect a kid's sense of self, like you don't want to make them feel like they are lesser than the other kids.

—I don't know though. I don't like disabled either, I mean, how can a ten-year-old not feel weird being called disabled?

—I like differently abled.

—Jesus, I fucking hate that one!

—Shh.

—*Differently abled.* Fuck you. I know I'm disabled. Don't take that away.

What? There might be more. I'm sure. The hushed tones make it hard. I hear more, here are snippets. It's not enough. I give up. I roam. Always roaming.

—Spare change?

—Don't you bitches watch where you're going?

—It's kind of fun to walk on the road like this.

—God bless you!

—Fuck I'm hungry.

—When does the stuff start?

—It starts at sunset.

—Yeah but when?

—Sunset. Jesus.
—I hope it's better than last year.
—I didn't get to go last year.
—Last year everything was shit.
—It isn't like it used to be.
—They lost their sponsors.
—Nothing's like it used to be.
—Doesn't it bother you, people, to see someone on the ground!?

Later I settle, far from the libraries. Different crowd. Smoky smell, throbbing music turns meaning to nonsense. My reality falls out of shape. Interest and intuition over clarity. I'm going to get things wrong.

—So, there was this couple, right? They are dragons.
—Right.
—And then the officiator at their wedding finds her legs off.
—Where did you read this?
—I can't remember. Fuzzfeed maybe?
—Okay.
—So, the officiator has to leave, right? She has to take her legs home.
—Okay.
—But it the caterer is also an orifice. She does it instead.
—That's fucky.

What? Straining. Pressure headache begins to rise like a kettle boiling, makes the joke of technology pretending to be his other ear whistle.

Rain becomes white noise behind the glass bus stop. One person is sitting near. Do my best. Try. Half-conversation down phonelines build a world. How was school?

—Because I got the machine call again.
—Oh.
—It was okay. I'll be home soon; I'm just getting on the bus.
—It's in the fridge.
—Anything else?
—Okay.
—Dog food.
—Okay.
—Love you, sweetie.
—Okay.

Slow sad beep, downward twang of a dying battery. Silence. Dead hearing aids separate us. The bus comes, a woman gets on. There is nothing else to hear. Wind touches my face, it makes no noise.

—What?

***Ben Berman Ghan** is a writer, editor, and incoming PhD student at the University of Calgary. He is the author of* What We See in the Smoke *(2019) and* Visitation Seeds *(2020).*

the miracles that don't show up

Walking in the sunset that had a sudden glow to it made him remember this was not the only time a light like that would form, *but it would happen forever and ever, an infinite number of evenings.* When I have looked at you, such a light could be there and all I can think is the many years, decades, we did not know each other and how those aeons of time *without borders* are a gulf that cannot be bridged, like *dream interpretation*. The sheer distance involved, the huge chasm below that gapes like the Grand Canyon where I hear people fall in all the time. Wayfarers and tourists take one step too far in their efforts to picture themselves on the precipice of danger with the courage of foolhardiness. But all I can think of is how unfamiliar the world has become, how strange and foreign my own life seems, with the *dusty, cluttered corridors* of our lives, the *kaleidoscopic distractions* and displays of ephemera along the thresholds of doorways, knowing if we had crossed paths long ago we may have walked past each other without a single blink of recognition. There would have been no mutual understanding, no fall into unknowing, and I would never have learned to *lean my starving body against the sun.*

I feel the rose keep opening

He says *we saunter toward the Holy Land* when we walk. Then one day the sun will be brighter than it has ever been before. But in this house, in the end, I stand by a white radiator where the sun sends its rays at noon from the window gently onto the surface of warm pipes and a brown floor. I stand still now, with no special feelings except a lingering ambiguity that seems woven into the cashmere fabric and soft silk threads around me. We both know the power of Tibet, the proud innocence, the victories of lovers. The magical talisman, the spirit that subjugates the heart. A gold sculpture from antiquity with raised hands stands facing me and out of the sides of a red lacquer bowl prayer beads tumble out, gleaming in soft sunlight, with two brass bowls, one on each side, there for balance. I wonder why there is no tranquility after all, why it all seems just a *useless burden*, a hope and a prayer in the early afternoon. I keep thinking about the words we have read together in the early dawn: how *it will take longer to erase the self from memory than it takes for bones to disappear in their graves.* And just as with a sudden sandstorm bursting up on a dry path, *I will learn to forgive this dream.*

***Kristjana Gunnars** is a writer and painter living in B.C. Her latest book is* Scent of Light *from Coach House Books, 2022.*

KERRY HALE

St. Kateri, Lily of the Mohawks

The day the church was razed, the face of St. Kateri Tekakwitha shone. A weathered hand reached into the rubble and plucked the godly image with revelation and an audible gasp. Nearby, those who stood knee-deep in ash and ruin turned to look across at the picture in the old lady's hands. It seemed proof enough of something. Where once the church stood white and octagonal, windowpanes layered in decades of brushstrokes and hypocrisy, a wide hemlock double door, a cross that cast toward the heavens a cold call to Christ-His-Saviour-Amen, there was now nothing. Outside, in invisible plots, the sanctimonious resting places of the kids that never escaped, guarded by the holy spirit, and, further still, shattered relatives torn between promises of the gospel and the truths of cultural pillage. The most recent blessings of communion held just yesterday in the church; before that a baptism, a confirmation, pronouncements as if to subdue and eradicate. "It's not God," the steadfast muttered, "but the people who worked there." To appease, traditional ceremonies were accepted into method of prayer, smudging, sweetgrass, sweat lodge, an interconnection, but the sacrosanct converts turned away. Turned away long enough for the match-strike and the godly kindling to ignite and the epicentre of faith—that century-old monolith of sorrow and hope and suffering—to torch loud fiery flames and cinders that plumed heaven-bound in retribution. Everything burned. Walls ashen, bell melted, the ghastly cross no more. Everything burned. Arsonists, traumatized and proud, crept into the night. But the weathered hand of the old one reached and plucked from the anguish that photograph of St. Kateri

Tekakwitha, Lily of the Mohawks, baptized as Catherine. Face scarred by smallpox but smoothed at death in miracle, now vibrant in colour photo. Black hair flowing, eyes dark and unwavering, Mohawk gown majestic, fingers interlocked at heart, the old lady whose hand held it whispered, "It's the message" to those nearby disciples, and faith —amidst ruin and in customary deference—was restored.

Originally from The Great Southern Land and now residing in K'omox territory on Vancouver Island, ***Kerry Hale*** *finds literary inspiration in sunrises, birdsong, indigenous history, and coffee beans.*

JOTI HEIR

Gigglers Deserve Daffodils

The people in the window were staring at me. Three of them had their noses pressed against the glass. It was quite unsanitary. I was watering daffodils with a dropper. That's when a bomb went off in my head. I think it was because I heard a giggle from my bedroom. Bedrooms are indeed supposed to have giggles. Sweet, soft giggles should come from rooms with beds. Sometimes even from under sheets on beds in rooms.

But you see, the thing was that I wasn't in my bedroom during the giggle and it made me feel a little scared and that is why a bomb went off in my head. I continued to water the daffodils because that is what a person does when they like to water things.

I lifted my hand to scratch my nose but it wouldn't lift. How absurd. So I tried the other hand. Same thing. Doubly absurd. I wanted to know what it could feel like to giggle in someone else's room. But first these hands. I looked down and saw that someone had tied them down. The man in the middle had the largest nose, it was probably him. He would probably lie about it. He'd probably also lie and say he wasn't a Pinocchio.

The scent of the flowers had changed since I started feeding them waterfall water. I could smell their happiness. The freshly-cut grass smelled beautiful too, but there was a hint of anger. She was mad because I wasn't feeding her waterfall water too. I had forgotten to lay down my kneeling pad so my boring knees had a lovely green criss-cross pattern on them.

I rubbed my face in the grass too. My face was just so uninteresting. That's why bad things happen, uneven distribution of beautiful things. Why didn't our skin have more interesting patterns on it? I mean if lines must appear as we elder, the least they could do is be interesting. I wondered if the giggler had face lines.

It would be kind of hard not to. The only way you could avoid getting lines in the face was if you never smiled or frowned. For that to happen you would need to be dead.

People that giggle in other people's rooms should be dead, I think.

And I think, if I were to be able to make someone dead for giggling then I would bring daffodils to their funeral. Well, the daffodils were watered now. And I could go check on the giggler. I picked a few daffodils just in case.

The people's eyes opened wide when a man came into the room. Some of them lifted their lips from their toes. The man's lips seemed to have disappeared. His eyes were not wide-open, just regular open.

"Please good sir, did the giggler receive the daffodils?"

I'm not sure he understood. Or maybe he couldn't answer because he had no lips.

Soft Power

I was shopping in a large grocery store on an empty stomach when before me appeared four bowls covered by a clear dome. Inside the bowls were rectangular vanilla and chocolate wafer cookies with sprinkles. I looked at the sign next to the domed cookies and indeed these cookies were for customers. I always feel shy taking free food but I did not feel shy at that moment.

I went to remove the dome of the cookies. The dome was as likely to move as I was to fly. I noticed a crank at the side of the dome which asked for turning. Upon turning it clear tubes popped up in each of the cookie bowls. The tubes whacked the cookies into smaller pieces. A little hole opened up at the top of the dome and the tubes brought the cookie bits up to the hole and spat them out.

I grabbed as many cookie bits as I could before they hit the ground. I wondered why someone had decided to serve cookies to customers in this way. My tongue tingled in pleasure with the insertion of the first cookie bit. The next moment my ears shivered in distaste as a whole whack of children descended on the cookie dome.

They cranked the handle, knocked on the dome, yelled at each other, shook the tubes and went bonkers. A proper woman dressed in a smart blue skirt and shirt ensemble arrived upon the scene. She walked over to the children and said, "No, don't do that, you are not allowed to do that."

They all looked at her while chewing. She calmly removed a child sitting on top of the dome. I gave her a smile when she looked over.

"I really never know how to handle these kids," she said.

"Well I think you certainly know how to handle them now, bravo to you," I said.

As I walked to the checkout a wave of water smashed through the store windows. Panic ensued as it should in such situations. People screamed and cried and most of all they ran. The proper woman appeared waving a turquoise and navy running shoe and dashed after a man who seemed to be the owner. It was a lovely shoe.

The proper woman slipped and fell. The children saw her struggle and laughed. They then began a cookie assault. She shielded herself with the shoe before throwing it at the children.

"Citizen's arrest," yelled a man wearing an official-looking uniform.

He grabbed the woman and put her hands behind her back. The woman's eyes bulged out of her head and she began to laugh. She had a very wide mouth for a proper woman.

One of the children, the one she had calmly removed from the top of the dome gently tossed cookie bits into her mouth. She chewed them almost demurely.

Joti Heir *is a writer and journalist from Toronto. She has been exploring humanness while living and writing in Istanbul, Rome and most recently Kyiv.*

KEVIN ANDREW HESLOP

vignette in water applied by paintbrush to concrete on a hot day

"—with which—along with their encased instruments—the cargo hold is filled geometrically, doing what professional sports players—some think of themselves as 'sports artists' or simply 'artists'—call visualization: feeling, in their hands and fingers' twitch fibres, eminent phrases' patterns. They are wearing what to an American eye might be called 'sweatsuits' (although not matching as they don't think of themselves as that kind of unit). Most of them awake. Four in plateaus of differing depths of the condition of bodymind that typically recurs for several hours every night in which the nervous system is relatively inactive; their eyes closed; their postural muscles maintaining a position as near to supine as the airliner's manufacturer's lead mechanical engineer—in concert with aeronautical engineers and a small forge of analysts whose job consisted essentially of maximally economical human Tetris—has allowed their seats to be.

"The snare drummer is sitting in a row to himself in the back of the plane with a strap around his right knee attached to an octagonal practice pad which would have read Vic Firth on the matte-grey texturized rubber of the pad itself were it not so well worn, like the pad's centre which reads like a sort of cataract of faithful wear: they are playing with sticks and the polyrhythmic complexity of the second movement's transitory phrase before the third movement's beginning in what is effectively a duet for snare drum and piccolo, the density of whose notes on paper tend to give this snare drummer a not-uncommon headache, such that they tended to memorize their part as soon as possible, often by ear to avoid consultation of the sheet music, which functions, as for many percussionists, simply as a means to count the bars in which they're not actively playing like someone else's calendar in the month of a shared vacation.

"The piccolo player across the aisle is polishing the silver metalwork in her lap piece by piece, exhaling the moisture of her breath with intention and scrutiny and working the detailedly pulleyed arms and keys and embouchure hole until it gleams and she returns it to the hard black plastic case whose interior topography of customized green felt is a metaphor she snaps closed and slips into the mesh—she's one of the few musicians who is permitted the option of sitting with their instruments rather than storing them in the luggage hold—of the back of the seat of the french horn player before her. Not thinking of her part: she is thinking of the grandfather she has left sick in the hospital in Lisbon, wondering whether she is flying in a state of disgrace, whether she's a *bad granddaughter*—whether, if he survives, he'll forgive her and understand. She is telling herself he will, that this is what he would want for her—for her to be flying rain-streaked at nearly 600 mph towards the consummation of her dream—as she shakes her head absent-mindedly when asked by the attendant pushing the trolley before calling her back and stage-whispering *vodka cran.*"

portrait of a notable figure as conflated in my memory with another

"Sprigs of fir and cinnamon—he must have taped them to the sill—not so much a scent as a presence in the room—so the incoming drafts of summer night would be infused as they bent to the pages before which he—his arm invoking geometry and flattened to the desk—is sitting. It is late. He looks up. 11:56 p.m., he notices. *Dang nabbit,* he might be saying, the phrase wholly incongruous to his Polish ear at Berkeley, straining to acquaint itself with the rhythm of the parlance of the day. *For Pete's sake,* I imagine him saying, chastening himself for not having the thing into shape by now. *Pull your self together.*

"At this age, the regal bluffs of his eyebrows already overinterpreting their place in the play, like doorknobs which seem to think they're pistols on the mantelpiece. Swept back. Insinuating the majesty of birdwings, those slight frames on which all of the sky and the endless, variegated space beyond might sit. *Honest to Moses*, he mutters almost without thinking. The finite sky, biddable and clear, beneath. A state of suspension in his verses—of the world, yes, but—of the present moment, an invocation of the jars of pickled preserves, of onion, of garlic, of wild carrot, of cloves sitting row after row his aunts woke early to be up all day doing, denuding the passage of time of its relevance with the shrug of a jar's shoulder. I have it somewhere that *he is slicing pieces of the fatty, Baltic fish,* that he loved preparing herring on winter nights, had a touch of sentimentality for the Christmas season. Once—I hadn't known he knew the song—he sang 'Rudolph the

Red-Nosed Reindeer' for my four-year-old—he must have prepared it—replete with little impromptu fits of choreography. It was quite a thing to see.

"There's a certain angle at which the hands of a fundamentally good person come in to grasp, with their thumbs, the feet of the toddler in the high-chair before them. Something about the holding and the letting go—the rhythm of it—which identifies itself as the visible emanations of the soul. *Beyond a reasonable doubt*, he tries the phrase, weighting the word *doubt* with a gesture involving a clasped hand. *Raining both cats* and *dogs*, he practices saying in a mixture of bemusement and befuddlement at the peculiarities of this language he is becoming. Such that if you ever wish to discover the character of a person, observe them in the company of children.

"He and the hardwood creak as he stands pushing the palms of his hands through his lower back in a practiced gesture meant to lengthen the space between the lumbar vertebrae and to loosen the joints of the bowl of the pelvis itself. Then, walking out of the office with its sectional glass door, retrieving the key from his pocket. Locking it, looking towards the stair. *Slippers off*, he says, *by twelve ten*."

impressionistic ne'er-do-well bags the salmon's hammer: or, a portrait of a man about dawn

"Invaginate volunteer beans open and honest as sea-borne afternoons. Say they caught a charter. Say the man sold candied salmon at the market Saturdays. Say, when he shook hands, he transferred scales. Say he dreamt of poker games with pelicans. Say he dreamt of drowning—relished it—the lone feign of his falling body sending the jewels of his breath like boxcars to their breaking on the solid surface boiling to sinew like carcal epidermal layers on the spit. Woke with the taste of salt. The taste of salt a currency, a common sense. *The drum of shark-liver oil no worse than the hours that they rose.* They rose at oh three five six. Fifteen minutes to the dock by foot. It is a truth—It is a truth universally observed that needless talk is frowned upon on the water. Nearly two hours before the sun would rise its waking, this was so. Men greet men wordlessly in the dark: they go about their functions smooth as eels. The ropes, the nets, the poles, the tackle, bait, the fuel, the water, packs, the cooler and the throttle: it wasn't until they were on the water finding pace the charter said, *You boys sleep?* Affirmatives. *Good,* he said. *That's good.* Downriggers, weights, the city smell behind them; fresh and sharp and soft the sea before them. Not one of them thinking about the Rime of the Ancient Mariner. *As idle as a painted ship / Upon a painted ocean. Cholic*, the doctor would explain. He wasn't asked to spell it. The shark-liver no worse than rising at the hours they rose. Barefoot in the dream. The rough boat-bottom: he's paddling standing—the canoe isn't there—standing in water a mile deep, paddling harder and harder; the water rising,

rising past his knees, rising—harder, harder—his waist—the paddle up over his shoulders now. This is a man; this is a man. It is a truth universally observed. His sternum, his shoulders. He is paddling. This is a man; this is a m—."

anagram in nine instances from which more should have been removed

"Straining and struggling against the cordage of the moment, like Odysseus lashed to the mast, to be born. *Censure* is the verb that is getting us there: it was only in the poems that the faces of his sailors were *stoic*. This was Job-song. Part god, part agony, he would have felt the friction of the cordage; his skulls' sides temples at mute war. A moment wants a vice that way. *Take me to the rocks,* it says. *Give me the grave of the sea. Listen not,* he would have said, preparing his sailors, Ischia cresting, *to the man, the thing, which screams you otherwise.*

"It was the screams they heard first, entering the building. Locked playhouse. They kept the children in the orchestral pit. Architecture praised in the journals of the day for its acoustics. At first, a low thrumming, keening, indeterminate but vile in the bones' sank marrow at the breadth of it. It took longer than he thought it would for the chains on the doors to be cut. Minutes. The welder had used the phrase *case-hardened steel.* He was an underwater specialist concerned about friction without thermally-dispersive water at fission-point. The artifice, its audience sat in their container, night after night, row on row, dense as scales from the foot of the stage where it juts—*thrusts,* they say—into the shape of the world—the scales of riverfish as in Dominik's poem in which the northern lights are reflected there—desperate to be born. Out of love with being. Ragged with excuses. *Give us the supple make-believe, transient as tropical breezes, as sonatas,* they would say. *Bent as tempests,* they would say.

"It must have been raining, wind thrashing him, his hair medusal and animate. *Please* would have been the refrain. Or not: perhaps the tack was that of command, of authority, of violence.

"The scent flung from the tornadoed lavender-beds the monks walked sent a shimmer for days into two adjacent villages whose lovers gifted it bundled dry to one another. Sénanque Abbey. Generations of them.

"The cut chain had six times enwebbed the Halls' handles—returned as if in reverie: *If you too could pace behind the wagon that we flung him in*—flung open. Proscenium arch. Thrust stage. *They're beneath the boards*, someone had said. *The pit*, someone had said. The look of disbelief in the once-sullied cheeks of them, detectives in the wallows.

"Forensic the blood-spatter of siren song.

"Give me tango and timbre.

"Willing to have the wool pulled, they would stand in the rain with their umbrellas and not their umbrellas for the chance. It was a transportation we had been sold in the riddles and the anagrams of ruined myth.

"Straining against the cordage of time's encasement; sap globule running burly and courage—call it Jericho—along the ancient bark. *Like dogs. Worse.* They were in the pit, had been fed fast food. Wrappers and feces and vomit and vile beyond imagining. *They're under the boards,* someone had said. *They're under the boards.*"

***Kevin Andrew Heslop** is a polydisciplinary doofus whose work has lately appeared with Gordon Hill Press, McIntosh Gallery, and the Toronto Short Film Festival.*

ROBERT HILLES

Tale of the Pink Puppet

The front door opens right into the living room. A fox sits in a rocking chair. Squirrels play the piano. All of this isn't visible from the street. He stands just inside the door.

Sense that? The fox asks for it can speak. In fact, the fox belongs more in this house than the man at the door. The man wears leather boots and has opened the door without knocking. He assumes this is his house.

Sense what? he asks.

That, the fox says.

Okay, the man says and considers going back outside and closing the door and then opening it again and trying a second time. He knows by now that often does the trick.

Don't do that, the fox says.

Why not?

Hear that rain? Hear the river? Hear all that water? That is your doing. Why you are here now inside this house.

This isn't my house?

No. It was never your house, the fox says and gets up from the chair and shakes the man's hand because he is the kind of fox that can do that. There is much that this fox can do that most foxes can't do.

How is that possible? the man asks.

It just is, the fox says. *Now let's go to the piano and later we'll turn off that water. (It is the water that brought you here. You had the sensation that you must turn it off). We must shoo the squirrels away from the piano.*

Then we will sit. Out the window in front of the piano there is such a view. There is much you and I need to discuss.

The man takes off his hat and coat and joins the fox at the piano which is now quiet. The squirrels are already gone. The fox can play the piano beautifully and at first the man just watches and listens, and then in time he finds his place in the music and puts his hands to the keys and he too plays beautifully. *This is not music?* he says and wishes to weep.

No, it isn't, the fox says. *It is the ribbon inside your soul coming loose. Wait a moment more, play a bit more, and then when you leave, all of this can go with you, even me.*

Tale of the Blue Bicycle

She owns a blue bicycle and rides it to work every day. She also rides it to visit friends and to go shopping for groceries. Today it's raining as she rides to work. She stops at a red light and a car pulls up beside her and the passenger window rolls down and a boy pops his head out and says, *You're wet.*

Then she hears, *Bobby,* and the window rolls up again. The boy is right, she is wet, but she lives in a part of the world where the rain is warm and refreshing. At the next light a large half-ton truck pulls up beside her. It's silver and has tinted windows and she can't see inside so glances only once in that direction. When she does the engine revs.

The light turns green the truck hurries away from her and she takes her time pedaling. In time she speeds up again and the views on either side of her change. On one side is a mountain range with a fir forest greening the base of it. On the other side is the Pacific Ocean, the air salty and thick and the more she pedals the more she tastes salt.

In time, she is no longer here. Not in any creepy way or due to harm or any mishap. Also, there is no blue bicycle except that it best depicts her soul or what she thinks of as the soul every living being has. She has ridden her soul and believed it carried her like a blue bicycle. She houses it and transports it as she imagines it transporting her now.

She takes her hands off the handlebars and lets the bicycle coast as though down a hill, except she is on the flat. Still, it coasts and goes on coasting as long as she holds her arms out like that buoyed on the air, and in time she is lifted and realizes that there is no blue bicycle only her in this place that can't be described.

Robert Hilles *has published twenty-four books. His latest novel is* Don't Hang Your Soul on That. *These are from a new book called* Pink Puppet.

Red to Pink

Red candy canes decorate the front steps. I have a similar stripe down my hair. I'm wearing my lucky red lumber jacket, coziest thing in the world. Wore it the day I applied to nine different hairdressers, afraid I shoulda taken the college course, not the high school co-op. But it was so much cheaper and I *always* knew I wanted to make people happier 'bout themselves.

I open the door that is wrapped up like a cherry present with a white bow.

When the cancer took my Nana's hair I was the one who gave her her first-ever manicure, taking my time, letting her savour the colours under the light, choosing between seven different pinks all nearly identical. I lit a vanilla candle that she called "that smelly thing" but then asked to keep, after. Now I play soft music when I come on Sundays. She pretends to ignore it. Relaxation music. Last month I started to do her makeup.

"Just a 'titch'," she says, "because I'm—mature. I don't want to look like a fancy lady."

Nana means prostitute and I hide my smile. Honestly, with my burgundy pashmina hijabbed nicely around her little bald head and my touch ups to her cheeks and ears ("Ears really show the age," she whispers), Nana's as cute as a button. I brush the pink on so softly—often no colour on it at all, using the wide brush because I know it feels nice.

She closes her eyes. I brush longer. She splays her hands out in front proudly (crooked fingers, age spots like islands on a map, raised veins like mountain ridges), peeks at her Pearl Ballerina nails, and smiles.

Jerri Jerreat*'s writing, from Anishinaabe, Haudenosaunee territory, appears in, among others:* Flyway: Journal of Writing & Environment, Feminine Collective, Yale Review Online, and The New Quarterly.

MARY KING

The Roaring Twenties

Everybody thought the Twenties would be Roaring because we were stupid and sick, but what nobody realized is that history never repeats itself. It just makes you think it does. When things really started to slide, I realized it; that every time, it's new. Every disappointment, every failure, it's new every time. And now, they were saying there was something in the air, or in the water. And there were nosebleeds, which kept happening to me, and which started out of nowhere, on one of those days we were waiting for the Twenties to start Roaring. We were stepping out of the movie theatre and you said hey, you're bleeding. And I was, all down the front of my blouse.

Those days were suspended and open, like something you shouldn't be looking at. Like an exposed organ. We ate through boxes of clementines, even when they became too sweet, fermenting in their own skins. We'd go out, then we'd come back, then we'd lie down. We avoided the news. We'd go to the park where the grass was so dead it was on its way to becoming something else. You'd say, we're just killing time. If my nose bled I'd say hey, I can walk it off. We'd spend the night drinking and passing out in the tight heat of our bedroom. We were crying, and laughing, and we were walking it off, this sickness and this stupidness that was waiting for things to get better.

Empty planes burned fuel above our heads. We'd listen for birds.

History says: *The Roaring Twenties refer to a time of prosperity and economic growth throughout most of the Western World.* Legends about buying cars or land for fifty bucks, things like that. People not left wanting. I saw a magazine cover recently that said: "Fifty Ways to Dress for the Decade."

It seemed now that the only people who understood where we were at were these loud guys, prowling around the streets in pickup trucks. They took their mufflers off. There'd be six pick up trucks driving the wrong way down the road. They'd stick their heads out their windows and yell at children, elderly people, just anyone outside. It was so loud it would scramble your thinking and leave you empty and alert. Even people walking dogs. The dogs' legs would buckle in fear at the sound and they'd bolt for the road, dragging their owner and themselves into oncoming traffic. My nose bled on my shirt when it happened to me.

My bloody shirts would be hanging on the rack by the open window. Moths would bat around our heads as we stuck to the mattress. Citrus peel lodged in your fingernails and you'd be pressing against my heart. Trucks backfiring like guns and someone screaming, somewhere. Dogs dodging cars. Like they did every night, our heartbeats asked about tomorrow, and like always, the night would tell us, maybe.

Mary King *is a writer and musician. Her writing has appeared in* Grain, filling Station, Canadian Dimension, *and* Sunday Night Bombers.

LINDA LAFORGE

How a Garden Comes to Die

Butterflies stopped fluttering into her flower garden. Her heart sank at their memory, brushing her shoulder, landing on her nose. She stopped using chemicals long ago. She signed petitions and voted green. Her voice was ignored so they will be seen nevermore.

When artist and writer ***Linda Laforge*** *isn't drawing caricatures, she's in her studio with office manager and cat, Winston. Her work contains themes of loss, with concerns for social and ecological balance.*

LYNN HUTCHINSON LEE

Breakfast at the Aristocrat Palace Executive Motor Motel

The smoke of the forest fires drove me south from Pickerel River. I left my lover back there. We'd broken up anyway, but he refused to leave. By the time I got to the outskirts of Parry Sound, night was coming on, and the only place with a vacancy sign, red and hissing, was the Aristocrat Palace Executive Motor Motel.

The motel had a tilting balcony and chipped concrete columns. Somebody was sweeping gravel into the darkness.

I was greeted by a woman with bare feet and glowing teeth. She promised a sumptuous breakfast cooked by Grandpa, and led me through a peeling hall. *Oops, there's Grandpa now,* she said, *bluejay naked climbing in the shower,* and through a door I saw Grandpa, bent, ancient, toothless, helped by a tall boy. As the water poured over him, Grandpa began a series of ritualistic gestures. *Hey, no peeking,* the woman said.

At the end of the parking lot I saw overflowing garbage bags and a butcher's block piled with road kill. An incinerator fire was burning. *That's where Grandpa does his cooking,* my host said. *Just you wait.* Laughing, she walked off and called back, *All will be revealed.*

The floor inside was littered with cockroach bodies living and dead. A lonely bed, high and narrow, teetered at the end of the long room. Grey carpet halfway up the walls. *I hate it here,* I said to the room. I thought of my lover yelling as I pulled away, and called him. He was somewhere on the highway in somebody's truck. I gave him the address.

* * *

We had to wrap our arms and legs around each other to keep from falling off the bed and landing on the cockroaches. I thought of the current running through the red hissing sign, running through our bodies, jolting our lives together.

At dawn I woke to a delicious smell. Later, a knock at the window, an enthusiastic announcement of breakfast. I stepped through the door, and my lover said, *Where are you,* and I said, *On the other side.* And he came through. *Everything's like the sunrise,* he said. *Primrose-coloured.* It was true. Even the walls were gold-washed, no longer pitted and peeling.

Grandpa stood over the incinerator, arms like wings in flight as he stirred and tossed, sliced and caressed, and mounds of wild onion tarts appeared on the platter, bowls of blackberries and plums, blue-shelled eggs, sauces and jams, ducklings stuffed with sorrel and forest leeks, and our host came up behind me and said through her luminous teeth, *What'd I tell ya?*

As my lover and I ate, the feast ignited the cells and tissues of our bodies—suddenly naked—an acknowledgement of what we might make of our braided lives, together or apart. *All is revealed.* The woman's voice laughing from the halls, my lover and I seeing each other river-deep, our sightlines travelling along a strange ancient love.

Past the Dump

It isn't easy getting through the snow to the dump in Jeppeson's woods. A new geography has grown up and around the car parts and tractor tires, hillocks covered with diapers, empty shampoo bottles, cans of spray paint: the little cousins of the Anthropocene. You dig and dig through the snow, searching, making little tunnels that collapse, but at the end there's always a surprise.

1.

Bedsprings slice through the snow, empty tin cans, a toilet tank. He falls reaching for a small red truck with missing wheels, and his snowsuit gets wet. He doesn't cry, but holds out the truck for me to see. I think I hear *Look, Mommy*. We go further, digging for more treasure.

Past the dump, through a slit in a wall of trees, we come to a wide path between looming dead pines. I can't remember seeing it before, although we've been here many times. The landscape is white and grey, drifting, stained without the stain being visible. I'm uncomfortable sensing the stain. My child drops the truck and doesn't pick it up. We're nervous going down the path between these trees because it feels deliberate, as if we're being directed. We long for the comfort of the woods back at the dump where there was no design or artifice to nudge us quietly down the dark path. *Can we go back?* I hear.

2.

Where the alley of trees ends, so ends the path. A few mounds under the snow. When walked on, the mounds are unstable. When one foot steps onto the glazed crust, the foot taking the next step plunges.

Another mound, further on, arouses our curiosity because it feels older. Touched by the stain of time and loss. Disturbed in an insubstantial way. We see an indentation like a small shallow tunnel, and take off our gloves to gently remove the snow and dead leaves from the entrance. It's hard to figure out what's inside, but as we slide our frozen fingers to part the twigs and ice, we see a baby.

It moves, lifts its head. The eyes watching us from the darkness of the tunnel. As we reach our hands forward to take the baby, bring it out to the warmth of our arms, it moves further back into the darkness until we can no longer see it. Pulled back into its tunnel as if by a string. Before it disappears the baby opens its mouth in a slow smile.

Lips pulling back over the teeth. Small, sharp. The mouth opens wider, but no sound.

3.

Everyone knew the story. The dump where it was told that the girl gave birth to her grandfather's baby and went back home with empty arms.

4.

In the silence I turn to my child. I want to say: *Let's go home now.* But he is no longer here.

Something Has Fallen In

I came home by way of the marsh, it was then that the wild orchids were in bloom, the lady's slipper, coral root, helleborine. All the fens and wet fields, the shores of the river, shady places, humming, chirping, blurred with blackflies and mosquito clouds.

I was coming down Government Road with my orchids, there was a black car, and the man stepped out and said *oh what lovely orchids.* He had rich man's teeth and beautiful fingernails. He let me sit beside him in the front seat while he waited for his fiancée. *What pretty slippers you have, little straps tied at the ankle.*

He asked to hold the orchids and I said yes. He'd never seen an orchid up close, he said, and laid them out like a sleeve along his arm. *Which do you like best?* he asked.

This one, I said, *the lady's slipper.* I folded my hands on my lap and waited.

Louise, he said, turning to me, explaining, he was waiting for Louise after her fitting, and then Louise called out *Darling* as she ran down the steps of Edna's Brides.

* * *

There are four ways to look at what he did.

The First. His one hand belonging to Louise, his other in the fold of my dress. His hand relaxes the fold, it isn't my fault, it's the fold that wanted to open.

The Second. The slippers are under glass in wooden drawers that glide out of their cabinet as if on wings. There are rows and rows of them side by side. Most the size of a sparrow's body. *Imagine having such a tiny foot.* He slides back the glass and lifts out a slipper. It's white with yellow stitching. He points to the flowers. Chrysanthemums, he says, handing it to me. Five hundred years old. A lady brings tea on a tray. *Thank you, Mrs. Hannah.* Mr. J. pours the tea into little white bowls and gives me one. He says it's chrysanthemum tea. *Like the shoes,* he says, *the lady's slippers.*

The Third. I'm afraid to drink the tea. I'm afraid to stay on the chair. Its legs are too thin and lacy to hold me. It's made for Louise, a light body. Where is Louise? Later we look at the slippers again. *You couldn't walk in such shoes.* His sleeve brushing my leg when he raises his bowl to drink. *Only be carried.* His hand's on my back and I turn. *Louise is gone,* he says.

Time swells, contracts; a muscle we can't feel or see. Nothing's concluded, nothing ends. The air cools itself, gathers. The orchids in the marsh, the earth black and crumbling, the front seat of the car, the hand touching the unsoiled orchid that was picked only half an hour ago.

The Fourth. Louise the bride jumped off the Plough River bridge, although some say she was pushed.

* * *

The lip of the orchid. Look. Something has fallen in.

EDITORS' CHOICE: SELECTED AS BEST FLASH

My Heart Alive As a Sand Fly in the Towering Wave

I was made to stand at the bottom of a cliff. The cliff, bristling with rusted car parts, tires, cedars, rose from a narrow shale beach, and the water was an ocean. Along the beach were the remains of a laptop, a satellite dish, half a car, shattered cellphones.

I was made to look at the place where the ocean and sky flowed into each other, the place where a wave swelled lightly. A tanker was out in that watery airy space. The tanker was of the same hue, although somewhat darker.

I was made to watch the point on the horizon where the wave gathered, and I saw the water tilt in one way, then another. I saw the tilt billow and grow, and I knew that the wave became aware of me standing there. Even so, my feet clamped tight to flattened water bottles, plastic bags, to the stones of the beach, the soles of my feet grinding the splintered shells, the pitted grey stones and the sharp ones.

The tanker listed and sank, its bow nodding at the sky.

I was made to follow the coming of the wave and then it was here, billowing, advancing, and I looked up and the wave was taller than the sky and wider than ten harbours.

I was made to feel the crashing of the wave, and as it descended, blackness.

I was made to know that after what may have been seconds or hours or days, something moved.

My skin palpated by salt air.

My heart alive as a sand fly.

Alive as a beetle, a root, as the cedars on the cliff. As the net of fibres connecting, merging, humming under the cedars, under the trees behind the cedars, the ones I couldn't see but knew were there, the fibres pushing themselves into my feet on the shale beach, the connective tissues entering all bodies, each a part of the other.

There was a giant relinquishing as in love.

Notes for an Anthem to be Sung Before or After Her Death

Hellohellohello singing down the steps, feet riding the air over a border of marigolds—my beautiful sister in her white dress and lipstick the colour of crushed tomatoes.

The broad steps. The shaved emerald lawn. The building like a castle in the movies. She turned and pointed to her window on the second floor and our father tilted his hat, smoothing the feathers, and fiddled with the car keys. He was there and not there. My mother unfurled a blanket over the grass and we sat.

My sister's dress billowed around her. It was polished cotton, and across the surface were pale yellow music notes. *It's my singing dress,* she said. My fingertips touched the edge of the skirt and it was like a melting glacier.

Then we ate lunch, cheeseburgers and French fries and tea from a thermos. A gust blew our father's hat and a feather detached itself, floating. My sister caught the feather. She put it into her cheeseburger and ate, looking at our father with her red smile.

A man like a movie star came down the wide steps to stand before us, and we got up, dazzled, still chewing and brushing off crumbs. He wore a white shirt that matched his teeth, and shook hands with our father but not my mother. *Why hello little girl,* he said to me, and then got down to business. His hands clung to each other as he spoke and his words smelled of electrical burning. I tasted the burning in my mouth.

My sister was over at the marigolds, picking like crazy. *Is this your castle?* I asked, and she laughed and said, *No, it's a five-star hotel.* Then

I asked, *Is that man your husband?* And she opened her bright lips and laughed louder. She said she'd teach me to blow smoke rings.

Then came a scream nobody heard. My mother and the movie star man went on talking, and our father dusted off his hat.

The scream came again. It didn't stop. It came from inside my sister even though she was smiling and laughing while our father and my mother kept nodding at the movie star man. *Okay Doctor,* I heard. The screaming smelled of metal doors and bleach.

A woman dressed like a nurse took my sister inside. Other people on the lawn were making gestures unfamiliar to me, and one of them came up to the car as we left and drove her face against the windshield. I turned around and my sister was waving from her window.

When we visited again she was wearing pyjamas, even though it was the middle of the day. She had made me a doll with a white dress of polished cotton and pale yellow music notes. She showed me the hole in her own dress where she'd taken out the fabric. She held out the doll. Her nail polish was chipped. Her burnt smile. No scream.

Lynn Hutchinson Lee's *writing appears in* Room; Wagtail: the Roma Women's Poetry Anthology *(Butcher's Dog, U.K.);* Food of My People *(Exile Editions); and other publications.*

Call Me Julie

"Call me Julie," the girl said through a wad of gum that smacked when she spoke. Pink-streaked hair, obviously a home job—or a street job, in her case. She clunked her dilapidated brown suitcase onto the floor and it sprang open, spewing a few thin shirts and a couple of tattered books. She crouched to shove the items back in, hauled on the rusted zipper, but it refused to budge. Frowning, she stood up, arms crossed as if I had said something insulting that she wouldn't dignify with a response.

I knew her name wasn't Julie, but I wrote it on the intake form anyway.

"Age?" I asked, perhaps a touch officiously. My knees ached from hours of standing and I felt faint from going too long without food. Retirement volunteering wasn't turning out the way Roshanda had promised. *You'll love it. Works like a charm for keeping you spry. And social.*

Maybe socializing with delinquent teens wasn't what she'd had in mind. As for staying spry, the burning in my knees begged to differ.

I tapped my pen on the counter while "Julie" considered the question. She peeled a crushed bubble from her lip and stuffed the gum back into her mouth. "Eighteen," she said. Her eyes never met mine; instead she glared at the anti-smoking poster below my window.

I passed her a pen through the sliding tray and slipped the bottom of the form under the glass, far enough for her to sign.

"No, thanks." She dismissed them with a languid wave, but her eyes flashed.

I gritted my teeth, remembering my own attitude the first time I walked through these doors, feeling as if I were walking naked across a crowded room, every set of eyes drilling into me. Fifty years ago now. The building smelled exactly the same, brisk cleaning fluids and stale food, staunch hope and stark despair.

The posters were new. And the glass. Maybe they put that in after my one-time friend Max put a knife to the receptionist's throat. Max was dead now, his face a blur in my memory.

"You can't stay here if you don't sign the rules," I told the girl.

She shrugged, eyes once again placid. "Okay. I won't stay here then." She picked up her suitcase, cradling it in both arms to keep it from spilling its contents again. But she didn't move her feet.

She wanted a challenge, to see if I cared enough to make her stay. I pulled the paper back inside and turned it around.

"Okay, Julie," I said with sarcastic emphasis on the name. "Thanks for signing."

Eyes startled, she opened her mouth. Before she could get a word out, I scrawled *Julie* on the dotted line.

"Here's your copy. Read it." I pushed a duplicate at her.

She closed her mouth and took the paper. For a moment, her gaze met mine. It may have just been the bright lights, but her eyes seemed to glisten.

Razor Wire

All Maggie wants is a slice of apple pie, a shower, and a nap. She heaves herself off her mother's sagging paisley couch, her black workpants like canvas around her legs, cargo pockets on either side for her handheld radio, notebook, and spare pens. Paraphernalia for walking the perimeter of the substation outside of town. Maggie's presence ensures no one steals the copper from inside the razor-wire fence. In the three months since she started this gig, she hasn't spotted anything remotely like a human form, although she does sometimes see squirrels perched on the fence, paws on the razor wire as if they own the place.

She cuts a slice of pie, as her mother's footsteps pad down the hall into the bathroom. Taps run, the toilet flushes. Same routine as yesterday, and the day before, and every day before that.

"Morning, Mom," Maggie says when her mother shuffles into the kitchen, hugging her frayed housecoat around her waning body.

"Pie for breakfast again?" her mother says.

Maggie takes a bite, swallowing a retort.

"I see you left it on the counter." Her mother scrunches her face.

Maggie stuffs the rest of the pie in her mouth. Its former sweetness tastes like glue. Without responding, she stomps off to her bedroom like a teenager, wishing for the hundredth time that she hadn't moved back home.

"Huffy, are we?"

Her mother has followed her. Maggie swings around and glares. The shock on her mother's face flares like a beacon warning sailors away from submerged rocks.

"Margaret, I've just about had enough of your rudeness." Her mother's voice pitches low. "You know I do so much for you, because I love you. I can't be tiptoeing around your moods."

Outrage surges through Maggie, blackening her vision and clutching her throat like an assassin. She wants to punch a hole in her mother's drywall.

Two hours later, fat drops of rain pound the house. They plunk into Maggie's hair as she loads the last box into her car. Her hand is steady as she turns the key in the ignition.

Marion Lougheed *grew up in Canada, Benin, Belgium, and Germany. Her flash fiction shortlisted in the 2021 Sunlight Press Flash Fiction Contest. Tweets @MarionLougheed.*

LORETTE C. LUZAJIC

Peppermint Bay

You were threatening to kill yourself again, so I turned back inside myself and stepped aside. I didn't have the brass to buoy your burdens, or to bury them beneath the debris of where we'd been and what we'd seen. I just wanted you to stop pretending your pain was the only kind that mattered. When the noise inside me got so bad I wondered if I would split apart, I would walk down towards the water and pluck peppermint from the sprawling garden. Give me one reason, you said so many times. This leaf, I said once, holding a sprig to sniff. The clean, acerbic bouquet of it always held some clarity. This newt, I say now, nudging nearer to the wee beast's hiding place for a better view. Once Daddy caught one for us while chopping firewood, held the squirming eft in his cupped hands so we could see it closer. Said some kinds of salamanders could carry on even if they lost a foot or tail to predators or danger. They grew another one and got on with it, he said. I looked up then to Daddy's face for a tell, not sure if this regeneration story was him pulling our leg. And your voice, cutting into the moment and taking all its magic. *Why would the stupid lizard do that?* you asked. *He never asked to be born in the first place.* I wanted to wipe off your pout even back then, but you stomped off and Daddy dropped everything to run after you. Now I watch it again, the little red saurian scurrying to cover. Think, how valiant his small scramble for life.

Lorette C. Luzajic *creates collage paintings, writes small stories and prose poetry, and edits* The Ekphrastic Review, *a journal of literature inspired by visual art.*

WENDY MACINTYRE

Shadow

I read that in Colombia there is a sniffer dog named Shadow so skilled in detecting cocaine, drug smugglers have put a bounty on his head. I wonder if he is a German Shepherd, and what colour his fur is. I would like to know if he is aware, out of some superlative canine instinct, that he is marked, the constant target of desperate men. I wonder if he twitches in his sleep, if his dreams are haunted by two-footed creatures adept at murder.

I want him to have a particular handler who holds him in affection and esteem, who does not see him solely as a tool for enforcing laws. I want him to be safe, and sometimes to be allowed free play, bounding after a flung stick or ball. I want them to be sure to check his food for poison.

You did not want us to have a dog. You said they were messy, smelly and demanding, that their fawning attachment filled you with disgust. I think you feared bringing a dog's love into the house would reveal too starkly all we did not have.

Sometimes I get up during the night and go down to the kitchen, where I open the refrigerator to let the angled light illuminate the dark. I imagine an opened tin of dog food there, the kind with meaty chunks. I would like to say I feel the brush of his shadow against my bare legs as I stand in the refrigerator's glow, but it would not be true.

Simone Weil says we do not know when we do evil, because evil flies from the light. This is the kind of observation that enrages you because you say it is glyphic, slippery, and specious at root. As I stand in the refrigerator's light, I seem to grasp the whole of her meaning.

When you raise your voice at me, the dog would growl and bare his teeth.

He and I would come down together in the night, soft as shadows, and I would open the refrigerator, take out the can and put meat in his bowl. Nothing would please me more than his consumption of that food I knew to be safe and wholly nourishing. Then we would sit on the floor, quietly side by side, while I pondered Simone's insight and how it is we do things we do not know we do.

Wendy MacIntyre *is a Scots-born Canadian. She studied English Literature at the University of Edinburgh and has published five novels with Canadian independent literary presses.*

DARLENE MADOTT

The Window

"I wouldn't trust that, if I were you." The guest beside me at the cocktail reception leaned against the security railing. On the other side, only a six-foot drop, but one that if the railing gave way could do considerable damage. And suddenly, my drop into memory from the end of my legal career—to the trauma of being witness to something that happened when I was about to become an articling student.

I was there—there in the boardroom where students were being wooed with cocktails on the 52nd floor of a downtown Toronto Bank tower. Cocktail parties in the Bank tower law firms were occasions where students, good-looking on paper, could show off their social wares and articling committees got to see who did and didn't fit into the culture of their firm.

A partner with too many cocktails under his belt, three-sheets-to-the-wind, leapt onto the ledge to demonstrate his articling party trick. He hurled himself, shoulder first, with blind trust against the window. But this time was different! Caught by the wind, the window flew out like a sheet of ice and disappeared with the suited lawyer, his jacket and tie fluttering. The glass didn't shatter until it hit the ground, 52 stories below.

Those nearest the hole of the gaping window were sucked toward the void, but dropped to all fours and crawled without dignity toward the boardroom door. No one screamed. Only the wind made its whooshing sound.

The firm offered grief counselling.

"Don't Walk Barefoot"

(From the Instruction Manual for
"What To Do In Case of Hurricane,"
Paradisus Resort, Jamaica)

Just over twelve years ago, she finally found the will to leave the monster. It wasn't strength. It was not wanting the monster to do to her Benjamin what the monster did to Jane. "If you go to him, so help me God ..." Frozen with fear in bed at the monster's side, she listened to her baby wail. It was almost unbearable. And then it was. The monster stormed out of their bedroom, pulled the crying babe from the crib by the ears. *By the ears.* Because she had followed. Because she had watched. The monster tossed the child back into the crib and came after her. Later that night, the monster finally passed out in a drunken stupor. Her split mouth salty with dried blood, she clutched up Benjamin, now strangely silent though his little eyes were wide open, grabbed her purse and ran into the street in pajamas and bare feet, ran and ran to the nearest cop car idling in the parking lot of a Tim Horton's—the purse, in which she had three tampons, a single diaper, a tube of lipstick, fifty-five cents. No identification. The monster had taken that too.

Darlene Madott *is an award-winning author of nine books, including* Dying Times, *Exile, 2021.* Winners and Losers *is forthcoming with Guernica, 2023. More on Darlene at www.DarleneMadott.com.*

CARIN MAKUZ

Two and Two

You learn a lot about people running a motel in the middle of nowhere. There's a woman right now, checked in today, walking the field, round and round the edge of it, clockwise, been at it for an hour, sometimes flaps her arms like a bird. This is new, never had one like this before. She asked about the walking when she phoned for the room—is there a place to walk she said and I said, well, the husband takes the dogs out to the field, lets them run, they seem to like it. We're on seven acres I told her in case she thought we're some rinky-dink spit on the highway. The field's nothing much, a bit of scrub, room for the RV and a shed, I didn't mention that part. There's a tone to her voice I'm not crazy about. Anyway, I said yep, there's a place to walk and now here she is, going in a circle. Running this place thirty-one years and never seen anything like it. But this is how it is in the people business. Never a dull minute. Oh and the other thing ... she asked was anybody else staying here. I said of course there is, plenty, and she said she just thought because it was winter the place might be empty but I told her no, there's people come by all the time, got one staying 'til April in fact. *April* ... she said, *why's that?* and right then I knew she was from the city. People out here, country people, don't ask *why's that?* about personal matters. Anybody with half a brain can assume a number of things why somebody might book a highway motel room until April, it's not that difficult and anyway sometimes people volunteer the odd thing, you can put two and two together without sticking your nose in. Take the guy in #6 who broke up with his wife. I don't mind laying a bet it was down to a fondness for Johnnie Walker and friends because the places empties turn up you wouldn't believe. And Helen in the end unit who runs the bass fishing on the island where home help can't get to her convalescing hip. You don't have to be a genius to put two and two together and figure out none of her lazy ass kids can trouble themselves to lend her a hand. Then there's the woman who spends all day watching the free satellite and the couple whose luggage is a couple bags from Dollarama. Look, people want a room, can they pay up front? That's all you need to know. You don't ask *why's that?* Two and two. Put it together. You can usually take it from there.

I'll be honest with you though, I watch her circling that empty field round and round and I do wonder, I do.

And now she's flapping her arms again.

The Girl Across the Street

For years I've seen the girl across the street leave for school, running from her house like something set free.
But she's growing up.

Long legs now take slow measured steps like she knows what's waiting for her.

Carin Makuz *is the creator of* The Litter I See Project. *She lives in an old farmhouse on PEI where she walks red sand beaches.*

INGRID MCCARTHY

The Artist

Thérèse Coutu had given birth to three girls. When she was pregnant again, she hoped that this time, the Holy Virgin would listen to her prayers and not to someone else's lament and send her what she wanted: a boy.

And a boy it was. She promptly named him Jean-Marie. Then she kicked out her husband, *l'enfant de chienne*, for she had no more use for him.

Jean-Marie, her Ti-Jean, was a handsome lad. Thérèse paraded him around Sainte-Rose-du-Nord like a treasure received from the heavens above which in her eyes he was.

"He's going to be a famous painter," she told the neighbourhood women. "Like Picasso. And he'll be going to Paris, France."

As luck would have it, the boy showed signs of talent and Thérèse began saving every dollar she could spare. On his eighteenth birthday, Ti-Jean left for Montreal to enroll at École des Beaux-Arts.

Three years later, he returned to Sainte-Rose-du-Nord with a degree in his pocket but with grander ideas in his head.

"I'm not going to paint pictures and peddle them in the market," he announced to the protests and wailings of his mother and opened a tattoo parlour in the front room of their house.

It broke Thérèse's heart. In her mind, such art was common and vulgar. But soon, Thérèse's heart was on the mend again when she saw Ti-Jean's stunningly creative designs: fantasy animals and flowers, swirls and waves, hearts and crowns.

Men and women of all ages lined up to have their bodies tattooed, their payments lining Thérèse's pockets to the brim. Life was good again until Francine arrived on the scene and put Ti-Jean under a spell.

Francine was unattractive and, therefore, still unmarried at the age of thirty-one. But she had unblemished skin, so pale and creamy, he became obsessed with her, dreaming about her body that he wanted to possess and ultimately use as a canvas for his greatest work of art.

Francine had shown up at the parlour to pick up her brother who had his back tattooed with a fire-spewing dragon. When she placed the payment into Ti-Jean's hand and inadvertently grazed his wrist, the fire from the dragon's mouth had spilled over into Ti-Jean's heart, setting it aflame.

Thérèse sensed danger.

The following day, she intercepted Francine on her way to the market. "Don't ever come near my house again! Take this money and go away!" And, with that, she pressed a bundle of banknotes into Francine's hands, gave the unsuspecting woman a threatening glare then walked away.

Francine thought she'd won the lottery. She moved to Quebec City where she met and married a kind man.

The news that Francine had left the village drove Ti-Jean mad. In his deranged state of mind, he tattooed wherever his hands could reach every inch of his body with her name.

He neglected his business, and the business went out of business. In the end, Thérèse went mad as well.

After a 33-year career in the theatre, ***Ingrid McCarthy*** *now writes and publishes dramatic novels and novellas. Her latest publication is a post-WWII childhood memoir.*

NAELLE MCCORMICK

How to Fight Loneliness

They put all of her things in boxes a week or two ago, the lady across the street. Her porch was empty that day when I left for school. Workmen in thick wool coats muttered distastefully as I passed by, scowling at the arsenal of ceramic figurines now wrapped carefully in newspaper on her front lawn. She had sat still in her walker for nearly three days, scarlet evening gown bunched up around her knees, pearl necklace fallen into her lap. It wasn't unusual to see Ms. Byrne like this, slack jawed with a glass of brandy in her hand, and dressed to the nines on a Tuesday, Wednesday, or Thursday morning. Even in the winter, she seemed to rise the moment the dew wet the grass. Her legs had gone years before, and she couldn't hear all too well either. But Bridie Byrne hobbled outside impeccable each morning, hair crisp from overnight hot rollers and pale face glamorously made-up amidst harsh wrinkles. Though, if someone stepped closer, they might notice the ashtray loaded with damp Du Maurier butts, the blue shimmer tacked on up past her eyebrows, or the fact that she had long since taken her last breath. Perhaps no one had time for Old Ms. Byrne, save for tongue-in-cheek cruelties over foaming glasses of lager at the end of the week. Unknowing, she would grin at the laughter of the young reverberating off the walls of the well-lit homes. And all the while she sat, closing her eyes, night air silent except for the electric buzz of moths hurtling towards their ends. Only the hopeful missionary (who came days later), smiling ear to ear, feet light as air ready to preach the gospel of Jesus-Christ-his-Lord-and-Saviour-Amen noticed the soft bloat of her ringed fingers, the gentle cloud over her eyes. He turned, leaving the pamphlet at her feet, a sort of last-minute offering for St. Peter at the gates, I suppose. I grabbed it on my way to school the day they put up the For-Sale sign.

Naelle McCormick *is a Vancouver-based senior secondary student who writes about the mundanity of life's routines and expectations with grimy reflections on the human condition.*

DAVID MENEAR

Molten Bone

My hand so cold in yours I walk us silently through the cemetery of past loves and the tormented ghosts of lovers lost. There is no sky only empty white air shimmering.

We lay entwined denting the moist grass upon his shallow grave to make our own bed of blood. Hold me tighter you whisper into my 'good' ear—so tight that I can not breathe to speak of the truth of our lying again. Shunning others you allow your mystic self the incubus his ancient bruising weight of myth thrusting hard towards the shameless pleasures of beasts without blame suspended somehow writhing between your sleep and delicious dreams.

Gazing into the dry crying eyes of chiseled angels I say to you let us burn our bodies together into one of molten bone and glowing gray ash.

David Menear *lives between Toronto, Montreal & Divonne-Les-Bains. Now, in Toronto playing tennis with terrifying enthusiasm.* Swallows Playing Chicken *2019-2020 ReLit Awards finalist. David acts for film & television.*

DAWN MILLER

Pinball

I have moved into the last corner of my body. Thoughts ricochet against the confines of brain, my existence a tangle of dreams and memories.

"Peter."

A voice. Female. Unfamiliar.

"Just going to roll you onto your side. Put some salve on those bedsores." A string of sibilants, the faint hint of a lisp. She sucks in air, a soft whistle of exertion. Warm flesh presses—a forced intimacy—as she rolls me over and nudges me with her hip.

Tilt.

Vestibular fluid sloshes in the curved canals of my ears. Is that all? My body betrayed me long ago—synapses misfired, signals blocked—shutting off all the lights except those that remain in my subconscious.

The last thing I remember is driving on the interstate. The pressure of the clutch beneath my foot as I shifted gears.

All signs pointed to *Game Over.*

Yet here I am. The launcher full of hollow balls, the spring of the plunger pulled back.

"How's he doing today?"

A ball shoots out and bounces off a bumper.

Sara.

"It's been a rough night," the lisp says.

No, no, I want to say to Sara. Last night I dreamed we were canoeing—you in front. The water burst into diamonds as you dipped your oar, beads shimmering on the polished ash. We paddled for hours.

Tender wisps of damp hair clung to the nape of your neck. Your profile in laughter.

It was wonderful.

"I'm moving away, Pete," Sara whispers, a little catch in her voice. Her scent is like the beach. Sunshine. Vanilla. "I'll miss you. I'll visit when I can." Lips press my cheek; a strand of silky hair tickles my jaw.

If I could, I'd flash neon lights, set bells ringing. *Ding, ding, ding.* Let her know she deserves happiness. Instead, a heavy weight pulls me down, and I slip under.

Tonight, we'll head north of Wawa, drive down logging roads to find a level area and pitch our tent on a forest floor strewn with pine needles. Or perhaps we'll canoe to Crown Land, portage deep into the sun-dappled trees to a hidden gem with only stars and lapping water as company. Sara will wear those short-shorts I love, and I'll make a bonfire so tall the flames brush the cavernous arc of sky. We'll make love, tent flap unzipped, a cool breeze sending shivers down our limbs while across the lake, loons echo in a mournful chorus.

I can't move my limbs, my vocal cords are useless, my eyes remain shut. But I have harnessed my dreams, each one longer than the one before.

Given the chance, would I trade places with those who flit around me fussing with tubes and machines? Exchange this existence for a life of paycheques and schedules?

A futile question.

But I wonder sometimes, in those pinging moments after a thought rolls past the stilled flippers. Then I dream again.

Dawn Miller's *work appears in* Jellyfish Review, Typehouse Literary Magazine, The Main Review, *and others. To learn more, please visit www.dawnmillerwriter.com and Twitter @DawnFMiller1*

KATHARINE MUSSELLAM

Snap Back

She walks down the hallway and her mind is focused. She's looking for their meeting point, nothing more and nothing less. She does not think of the past. She feels calm.

Until she doesn't. She should have seen him by now. What's taking him? Did she come to the wrong place? She looks around until a short, loud sound behind her—

And now she's no longer living in the present. Just from that one little sound, she's somewhere else. She snaps back to when she was younger, to a more fearful time.

Funny how snap is a sound and an action, how the sound creates the action in her mind. She shudders as her head turns towards the noise, as she also wished it hadn't back then. She hates the way that sound commands her. How she had wished she could have resisted its power.

All at once, she anticipates the belittling and the yelling that she's wrong even when she hasn't yet been taught what's right, and after that some nitpick to ensure she's still wrong. If she asks a question, even the way she raises her hand will be a flaw worthy of condemnation.

She is brought back to that constant sense of never being enough no matter what she did, while others who worked as hard as her, did the same things she did, were pulled up onto pedestals above the fray. She is back to feeling like she did back then, sick of being considered less than, sick of walking on eggshells and too petrified to fight—and even if she did, she could never get a word in edgewise. She was only listened to when it was convenient or served some other goal. She doesn't know why she had wanted to be there until the day she broke. She doesn't know why she wanted the approval of someone who didn't think her self-worth was of any importance, didn't think of her students as anything more than servants to order around. Who'd said she'd respected her and then treated her like she had no feelings or independent thoughts.

She bristles, but she's also stronger now. At last, the words she wanted to say back then come forth to her lips.

"I'm not some animal!" she snaps—there's the other meaning of the word, the one she can use to fight back. She's not useless, and she won't cower from that fact. She deserves respect.

And there he is before her, slightly bewildered, but without his teeth pressed together to make the sharp shushing that used to always accompany the previous noise. That teacher is not here and does not have power over her anymore. Because this is now, not then.

"Oh," she says, back from the past. "Sorry. I just don't like that sound. Bad memories."

"Noted," he replies, a little shaken but not hostile.

No fight needed, she breathes an easy sigh.

"All right," she says. "Let's begin."

Katharine Mussellam *is a writer and cinephile from Markham, Ontario. This is her first publication in a flash fiction anthology.*

CAROL ANN PARCHEWSKY

Side Effects Aren't Optional

When I wake up I think of you. You are running through a meadow of flowers like in a pharmaceutical commercial. The side-effects drip across the screen like raindrops in spring smearing reality bending expectations. There is a scarlet flower missing a single petal. The petal was plucked by a teenager who said, he loves me. The teenager waits on a crowded platform for the morning train next to the yellow line. A stranger pushes the teenager forward over that line flailing onto the tracks. A scarlet puddle pools as the train screeches to a halt. The stranger was you.

Therapy

Bro, I wanted to update you on what I've been up to. I started running. Yeah, me, can you believe it? And not on a treadmill or around the block. In the eff-ing forest. Like a frigging gazelle. Okay, not quite, but close.

I like to run with someone slower than me, because, bears. Bears always catch the slowest. Then Tuesday, Scotty and Bryce couldn't make it, something urgent had come up at work. I didn't have that problem. I laced up my Solomons and hit the trails at Canmore Nordic Centre. Not many vehicles in the parking lot.

As I headed up Coyote, the trails always go up, I waited for the prize-winning fall views of golden tamarack. I felt like a frigging mountain man out there on my own with no tracks in the early morning dusting of snow. I should have been wearing a red and black lumberjack shirt.

At Meadow View, I stopped for a break to take in the view, not because my Achilles was screaming either. I sat on a rugged grey rock and watched the clouds glide past. The pungent steamy breath of an intruder permeated my space. I turned and looked over my right shoulder, a grizzly bathed in the reds and gold of the fall mountain colours stood, snorting. I smiled and said, "Hi George," knowing that I wouldn't have a chance of outrunning him.

I rather liked running on my own, or at least I thought I did until I met George. He turned out to be a good listener. I told him about me, and about you, the company, the arguments, the breakdown, the split, and all the in-between. Anything to keep him stopped, frozen in space, away from me. He exhaled or snorted when I paused in my narrative. He took my side when I told him about Glenrod vs Axelhood. Made it clear when his claws dug deep into the pine-needle crusted ground. I scratched his nose and gave him a hug when he affirmed my opinion. He hugged me back.

Oh, that's a picture of George, if you didn't figure it out. He'd do anything for me now.

I'd like my job back.

Carol Ann Parchewsky *holds an MFA from Queens University of Charlotte. Her writing has appeared in* Stanchion, On the Run, Flash Boulevard, Burningword Literary Journal.

TL PARRY-SANDS

Soulmates

The moment he saw her he knew. She gave him butterflies. She worked in a candy shop and she was as sweet as anything in the store. When he visited, she'd greet him with a smile and a candy sample—usually maple fudge. She'd noticed it was his favourite.

As his confidence grew, he visited the store more often. Whenever he bought anything, she'd sneak something extra into his little paper bag and draw a little flower before she tied it shut with the shimmery ribbon.

It was a Tuesday when he spoke to her. He thanked her for the treats and complimented her smile. He asked her out for a coffee.

"My treat," he said.

"I'm sorry," she said. "I can't date customers."

"Could I get a refund?"

At a café, under a red umbrella, on a folding chair, she sat with her hands in her lap. She laughed at his jokes, blushed when he smiled. When she reached for her coffee, he placed his hand over hers. Her eyes widened. She debated pulling it away but feared offending him. So, she used the other hand to sip her coffee. He had long fingers, impeccably groomed, and his skin was smooth, but her hand was beginning to sweat. She instinctively tried to break the grip but found that she couldn't.

When she glanced down at her enveloped hand, she found she couldn't tell his from hers. Terrified, she looked at his face. He smiled impossibly wide. Their arms had grown together. As she stood, her chair toppled and her coffee cup fell to the ground and shattered.

"Please," she said, pulling as hard as she could.

"You complete me."

He opened his impossibly wide mouth to swallow her. The fluttering in his belly stopped. He guessed it wasn't butterflies after all.

TL Parry-Sands *lives in Shelburne, Nova Scotia where she spends her time writing flash fiction and short stories, and working on opening her tiny bookstore.*

LISA PIKE

Ted & Sally

So it ended badly. A tragedy.

They went to the grocery store one day in Sudbury and Ted was driving in the oncoming lane so they had a head-on collision. Well, Sally got the worst of it. Ted wasn't so bad but he was in a different hospital than her. Not an asylum, but some place like that. It was then that they diagnosed him with the Alzheimers. All that year before he was acting funny. But it was more his personality than anything else. That was the year Henry and I had them in Florida at the trailer. They stayed with us two whole weeks and we treated them royally. Then, in the spring when we went up to see them in Sudbury, it was like he was mad, being kinda mean and ignoring us. So I said to Wanda, my sister, "What's wrong with Ted? It's like he's mad. I think that he's being rude after all we did for them in Florida." Little did we know it was the Alzheimers. Then he broke out of the hospital they had him in and he walked five miles or more in his bedclothes to where they had Sally in intensive care. But she never recovered from her injuries.

And that's ... what done him in.

***Lisa Pike** is the author of* My Grandmother's Pill *(Guernica Editions). Her poetry, fiction, and collaborative translations have been published in several magazines and anthologies.*

ELLIE PRESNER

Stung

Q: Is a picnic a good idea for a first date?

A: I wouldn't recommend this idea, because one or both of you could get stung by a wasp, in which case your (let's say it's a) finger will hurt like the worst fires of hell you can possibly imagine, and of course you don't have any ice cubes into which to plunge your poor fiery finger, so you hop around on the grass in agony swearing like a punk musician which will scare your date more than anything, as tears stream down your cheeks which you can't wipe up because you forgot to bring tissues, and the napkins (serviettes) are all stained with chicken fat from the sandwiches you won't get to finish since you now want to kill yourself because of the pain but you can't because the only knives available are plastic ones the deli gave you, but don't worry because tomorrow you'll feel much less pain but instead will experience the worst itching of your entire miserable existence and once again you'll wish you could somehow lose the offending finger, since you're positive you could get along just fine without it, even if you want to text the person you went on the picnic date with, which you don't because who the hell wants to be reminded of the worst pain you've ever suffered from in your whole life, well maybe except for childbirth, although that was a different kind of pain, horrendously whole-body-ish, whereas this is more like a razor-sharp spear ripping into your finger? Not me.

Ellie Presner *is a National Magazine Award nominee. Her books include a memoir of her stint as a script coordinator in the film biz.*

CONCETTA PRINCIPE

Nothing Is Missing

Listening to that magnolia in full bloom so weighted by the May snow fall it bends only so far then it cracks off. The third limb down in the frozen slush of a seasonal perversion. The conflict of too much, or something missing.

I have always thought of three as conflict or lack or something missing.

The three of a three-legged chair. Try to balance on that. Or, there is the triangle, a pretty stable form, if you get the long side loving gravity. Except the gravity of a love triangle. Ugh. Or the over-stabilizing 'third' wheel? In all cases three is a knife of conflict right up from the gut to the throat. Not as benign as the three-wheeled tricycle for children, learning how to graduate to two. A conflict of too much youth or not enough daring. Or the Trinity. Admit it, it's based on one sacrificing the other and from that wound, the third was formed, a.k.a the Holy Ghost. Conflicts everywhere. Trilogy. Just a story, you might say. Sure, but a story grows on conflict. Third place, as in bronze, or maybe just no cigar. Yes, the three of the Magnolia limb, sacrificed for the whole, a holy ghost. The Lack. Or a moment at which et cetera is acceptable … et cetera into the future.

This German Shepherd, missing a leg. With a three-legged gait he is so earnestly working with propulsion across the grassy lawn of the school. His owner throwing the ball and apologizing, periodically, for not making it go far enough. So sorry, Henry! The wagging tail, the mouth wide open with effort. Eyes and ears on the ball. Doesn't care about failures, just wants another chance. Give me the ball already.

Tail wagging his demand. Three-legged Henry may have balance issues at times, may never be as fast as his little heart wants him to be, may tumble sometimes, less often now that he knows how to live with his holy ghost of a limb, but oh his jouissance overcomes you, standing there on the other side of the chain link fence, watching his three legs holding the world together, as if movement hung on the force of ley lines, trajectories of heartbeat and delight, lace of his new life. Music for your eyes. Three as that which may bring you to this opportunity to try again, to run into your future with abandon, arriving where the world catches up with your reach. Nothing is missing in that.

Concetta Principe *writes poetry, non-fiction and scholarship. Palimpsest Press is publishing* Discipline n. v.: A Lyric Memoir *in spring 2023. She teaches at Trent University.*

KAREN SCHAUBER

A Real Doll

Candy red lipstick stains his starched white collar from left to right. It is clearly visible from meters away, but he bears no shame. The plump Russian belle who deposited the swak ekes out a high-pitched laugh as he pulls her toward him for a repeat performance. Whacking her behind, he announces brazenly, *My Prize*, and slips his stubby fingers deep into her cleavage to retrieve the shiny coin. Laughing that god-awful sound, she grabs it from him, and drops it in the slot setting the dials a-spinning. Her finger, fast to her lips, shushes everyone to listen for the *Double Diamond* payout. But there is no ding.

They've been partying hard since Tuesday. She's kicked off her ermine slippers and is bent over, looking for them. He takes in the view and smacks his lips, *Yum, Yum*. But the clock is ticking, and he knows it's time to pack it in. Summer's end is drawing near. Raking his hands through shiny cobalt hair, he pushes away the last dregs of beer and drags his coat up off the floor. *I've got to go, doll.*

The doll turns on a dime. It's as if he tossed her a stinger; her look, now bitter and dour. *Hey, where's my party girl gone*? He hands her the bucket, weighted with coin. It seems to appease, a bit.

A quick change into a clean shirt and he's motoring out of the lobby. No looking back. He fingers the smooth surface of the pink cockle shells in his coat pocket. The ones he picked up in the gift shop on the Strip, for his daughter. He'll tell her he found them at the seashore on his Faith Mission Retreat. Her smile, sweet, and innocent; she's Daddy's little doll.

Pushing the pedal to the metal of his luxury sedan, he hums a dandy tune. It's been drizzling on and off for hours and not much is visible. He makes haste. Salt Lake City is just over the horizon and his congregation awaits.

Sarabande

Ch'eng Mai lifts the violin from its case and drapes a chamois cloth over her shoulder. The notes ripple and bend like Hangzhou ribbon. She closes her eyes to better hear the Sarabande, its tone, tempo, and rhythm. And only then, when she is ready, does she pick up her bow.

Carnegie Hall is hushed in anticipation; every seat filled. The debut of this ingenue from abroad has been the talk of the town. Young aspiring musicians have flocked to hear the celebrated violinist. The tickets, a fortune; well worth the investment.

The piece begins with an exciting flourish. Ch'eng Mai adds florid elaboration to the slow pace of the harmonic movement. Her slender body sways gracefully as she pulls the bow across the fingerboard. Other times she is powerful and vexed, bending and twisting like a seizure. The display is riveting to watch; the music magnetic. Approaching the denouement, she keeps the ornamentation to a minimum, and the piece ends rich in mahogany tones.

The audience is on their feet, raving. Triumphant, Ch'eng Mai bows her head. Beads of sweat drip from her brow battering the stage like a timpani drum. It is her fifth consecutive performance this week. A grueling schedule for an eleven-year-old.

She steals a glance across the stage past her mother to Ling-Ling waiting in the wings. Her younger sister, prancing behind the heavy brocade curtains, clutches her favourite light-blue plush stuffy and sips fruity bubble tea; tapioca pearls dancing like maracas.

Moments elapse and the violinist is still standing with her head bowed. The clapping trails off, and the audience is quiet, confused, expectant.

Slowly, the violinist raises her left arm well above her head, and then, with a four-beat count, lets the priceless 18th century instrument crash to the stage floor. The gasps are audible, in unison, virulent. Murmurs, then chatter, splutter, cries, whoops, then shouts of Bravo, Brava, Bellissima resound.

The ingenue exits the stage, still, a hostage.

Karen Schauber's *work appears in seventy international literary magazines, journals, and anthologies. She curates Vancouver Flash Fiction—an online resource hub, and* Miramichi Flash—*a monthly flash fiction column.*

K.R. SEGRIFF

The Devil's Love Song

The Hilltop Pawn Shop's owner slithers his finger across the edge of Lu's guitar.

"I'll give ya fifty."

Fifty bucks doesn't seem much to Evelyn. Lu was no great hell, but when he'd played guitar, a sort of angel had shone out from beneath his layers of shit.

"Yes or no, Lady?"

Evelyn tells herself there's no sense getting weak in the knees about a loser whose only purpose in life was running White-Witch up to Waco. One thing Evelyn has learned in this crap life is that wants always kneel to needs.

"Sure. Fifty's good."

Mikey said Lu's last deal had gone south and his going underground was just business, but Evelyn had called bullshit.

Gone a month and not a damn word.

"That man's a rattler," Evelyn's mom had said. "Filled you with poison then left you for dead."

"You Evelyn?" the owner says.

"What the fuck's it to you?"

The owner reaches inside the guitar and pulls out a fat envelope addressed in Lu's unsteady hand. Evelyn is barely back on the sidewalk before she rips open the seal.

"It's the big one, Babe. Sets us up for life. But if things get hot, sell this blow to M and buy a ticket to Chihuahua. I'll wait."

When Mikey answers his cell phone, Evelyn stays silent. She promised Mom she'd never take the final fall.

"You there, Evie?" Mikey says. "You got something for me?"

Evelyn wants to stay motionless on the concrete until she comes to her senses, but her feet are already carrying her down the hill.

K.R. Segriff *is a Toronto-based writer and filmmaker. Her work has been published in* Greensboro Review, Malahat Review, *and* Prism International, *among others.*

LESLIE SHIMOTAKAHARA

Masset Inlet, 1922

I watch over this wild, green place. My father thinks *he's* the watchman, but where would he be if he didn't have me as his eyes? The good thing about being small is I can crouch low to the damp moss, as stealthy as a rabbit. Amidst these godly high trees, draped in glistening veils of lichens, I keep perfectly still, while they exhale their cool breath all over my skin.

I notice things. How the deer have gotten unnaturally big and bold, for instance. They breed like crazy, their offspring prancing around the razed areas of sun-bleached tree stumps, which look, from a distance, like whitened tombstones. Sadly, large sections of my lush fairyland have been reduced to such cemeteries. And men are discreetly packing up their families and gliding off in boats on the silvery water, a few more vanishing every day. Not just whites, but also Orientals; Chinese and Japanese, alike. Soon, me and my little sister may be the last Japanese girls around.

Yet Dad keeps his chin up. He seems to believe what the bosses tell him, that the boom can continue forever. I'm talking about the big American company that bought up this logging operation at the war's end. By then, these majestic spruces were no longer needed to build the Allies' fighter planes, over in Europe. When we first arrived, a giant raft of logs was bobbing forlornly, by the dock, no ship scheduled to come for it.

One afternoon, I'm standing on pebbly beach, watching the cumulus clouds gently drift and gather weight, when a bright flare ignites at the edge of my vision. A line of preternatural orange shoots across, travelling swiftly from the mill to the rooftops of bunkhouses. Fanned by the chilly breeze, the fire spreads eastward, and then men are tumbling out to the water's edge, buckets in hand. The womenfolk—my mother among them—aren't far behind, hauling furniture, setting it adrift on the waves, in attempt at salvage. Curtains of black smoke billow ghostly and slap at my cheeks, ashes raining down, like singed cherry blossom petals. Arcs of frigid drops cut through the doleful cries. Some kids and women clamber up a ladder to get on a docked ship, but I just stand there, incapable of moving.

When all is over, when all is burnt to a crisp, I can see what's going to happen. The last of the stragglers will hightail it, as fast as these nimble flames. But the watchman and his family won't go anywhere. I'll still be here, quietly keeping watch.

Leslie Shimotakahara *is author of two historical novels,* After the Bloom *and* Red Oblivion, *and an award-winning memoir,* The Reading List. *She lives in Toronto.*

J. J. STEINFELD

The Retired Break-and-Enter Man's Last Act

When was the last time he had plied his trade? the elderly man thought as he left his apartment, ready for his ritualistic Monday-morning walk to the liquor store for his weekly supply of medicine. He no longer had ambition or aspirations, he realized in a blunted, philosophical way, his meagre, solitary "retirement" little more than the cancellation of sanity and reality, achieved a few months ago without ceremony, this elderly man who barely made a sound during seven decades of rustling through all the noise and commotion around him. He was noticed by the young woman who lived on his floor in a building that would have been inconspicuous in another century or country but now attracted those that favoured the rearranging if not outright cancellation of sanity and reality. In the last week, two tenants had died of drug overdoses and a third was still in the hospital as the result of a botched suicide attempt, his half-page note with a half-dozen misspellings. A cynical sociologist might have called this the worst part of town, a shabby circle of Hell.

On many other occasions the young woman had seen the elderly man in the hall or in front of their building, and imagined he would be the perfect kindly grandfather, but only the slightest pleasantries or muted words were exchanged between them as if vindictive authorities might be listening. The elderly man was polite to a fault, displaying old-fashioned courteousness, never married, friendless, fearful of words, the briefest of conversations, head downcast, sometimes a slight knowing smile. He had spent time incarcerated in various jails and prisons around the country, but he always rebounded, mystic resilience, the new names he assumed helped, thirteen in seventy years, good or bad luck, not that he was superstitious, believing you make your own luck, create yourself, an inspired B-and-E artist as he liked to think of himself when he was younger and owned the town.

She a worn twenty, looking thirty, sobbing, had locked herself out of her apartment, and the elderly man stopped by her door, she apologizing to him and the world that cared nothing for her for locking herself out, for living her life of futility and confusion. Using a small knife he carried with him for memory's sake, with deft movements the elderly man opened the door for the young woman, his artistry reclaimed, her tears abated, offering a hug that felt like all the love in the world. She asked how he had done that saving magic trick, and with that slight knowing smile he whispered, *a lifetime of experience,* his heart turning on him in cruel trickery before he could devise a new name.

The Hydrologist

Wanting to ask a former professor of his to write an introduction to an academic book about coastal waterways and changing climatic conditions, a book he had nearly finished after five years of studying and researching climate change, the 63-year-old hydrologist went to the nursing home a five hours' drive from the university he had taught at for half of his life. The 63-year-old hydrologist couldn't believe what the administrator of the nursing home told him when he asked to see the 89-year-old former hydrology professor who had inspired his lifelong fascination with water when she supervised his doctoral thesis nearly forty years ago.

"She checked out last month," the administrator said and wrote down her forwarding address for the hydrologist.

Unable to contact his former professor, the hydrologist decided to take a chance and drive to his former professor's rural home, another three hours' drive from the nursing home. When the 89-year-old woman opened the door to her modest little rural home, the hydrologist asked if he could speak with her grandmother. "It's me, you old fool," she said. Believing he was humouring the woman, the hydrologist said, "You find the Fountain of Youth?"

"I didn't make a deal with the devil, if that's what you're thinking."

Over several glasses of wine, the former hydrology professor told the hydrologist about the magic powers of the river deep in the woods behind her ancestral house.

A week later, against his better judgement, the hydrologist ventured into the woods and cautiously waded into the river. He felt his body being pulled down, unable to fight off whatever was grasping him.

The hydrologist's body was never found, but the former professor seemed even younger, fulfilling her part of the bargain with the mysterious water creature living in the river.

Their First Full Meal on Earth

The three scientists, two men and a woman, one man just under 300 pounds and the other just over, and the woman a muscular 200 pounds—she had been a champion weightlifter before embarking on an illustrious scientific career—were honoured to be the initial selections to make historic first contact. The spacecraft landed on a sparsely populated island (now bustling with human activity and media commotion) in the Pacific Ocean a few days ago but translated messages had been received from space for months. The occupants of the spacecraft had informed Earth authorities that they had been studying with increasing interest Earth and its potential food supply. Strangely, the space travellers had requested large (by Earth standards) scientists to be the first humans to meet with them.

Full of awe and neuron-realigning trepidation, the three scientists entered the magnificent spacecraft, a modern-art version of a B-movie flying saucer and the size of a futuristic two-storey suburban house for a dysfunctional family of ten, as one wry commentator described it. Held back from the landing site by an international force of hundreds of fully armed military personnel was the largest gathering of the world's media ever in one location, jostling for advantageous positions to photograph and document the historic event. Several scuffles broke out among the media, quickly recorded and put online almost immediately, every picture or video or however garbled communication going viral in the blink of an extraterrestrial's eye. One of the reporters, camera in hand, broke through the military cordon and ran toward the spacecraft, snapping photos as he ran. At least a hundred bullets obliterated his body and journalistic career. The shooting increased the competitiveness among the media, the jostling turning into vicious shoving and unjournalistic bellicosity. The world was indeed watching. Everything around the spacecraft, however, seemed tranquil. Hours passed and no sign of the scientists or any of the space travellers, who had yet to make an appearance.

Afterward, one of the linguists working on the intergalactic translation project informed his superior of the latest intercepted message: *We were hungry after our nutrient- draining journey but a sample of life-sustaining Earth food has arrived.*

The Final E-mail of a Man Who Walks with a Cane

Hey, Sweetheart,

I just had to write you, tell you about how things were going. I hate that no-contact order. Not fair, not fair at all. I still have nightmares about how angry the judge was, lecturing me as if I was a stupid child. No damn contact whatsoever. Please don't report me.

I walk with a cane now. Crazy, isn't it? Remember my morning runs? I couldn't face the day unless I had those runs. Now they are just memory runs. Maybe I better explain. I was kicking and kicking at a concrete wall, seemed like a million times, trying to get my damn ankle monitor off, and completely wrecked my leg. What a joy, that electronic way of tracking me like I was some frightened animal in the woods running from hunters.

My first cane I got at the hospital but I found a beautiful wooden one at the second-hand store we used to go to. When I bought the cane, I had a gun with me. Hidden away, of course. But I thought about taking it out and refusing to pay. A robbery fantasy, I guess. Better than my porn fantasies, for sure. I did stop watching porn. I don't know if you're proud of me, but it's a weird accomplishment, wouldn't you say? I bought the gun the other day. I'm not scared or anything. I just wanted a gun. It was your cousin I bought the gun from. He's not in good shape, either. Way too many drugs.

After delaying and delaying, I finally did my will last week. Seemed like the right thing to do. Not that I have very much, but I'm leaving everything to you.

Speaking of not having much, the landlord is trying to evict me but I'm fighting that. A lousy apartment, but you couldn't get a much lower rent. And it's full of memories. The coffeemaker is in the will. When I used to come back from my morning face-the-world run, I'd make the best coffee for us. Two cups each, and we were off to the races. Not that you need or want a gun, but I'm leaving it to you, along with everything else.

I won't bother you anymore, but I'd sure appreciate a little reply, a few words to let me know how you're getting along in your new life. What a strange thing to write, your new life, but I wish I could magically create a new life, one without a cane or ankle monitor or no-contact order. I know if I had that new life, you would be my first and last thought.

Take care, Sweetheart, and please try to keep me somewhere in your heart and memory.

PEI fiction writer/playwright/poet ***J. J. Steinfeld*** *has published 23 books, including* Somewhat Absurd, Somehow Existential *(Poetry/Guernica Editions/2021) and* Acting on the Island *(Stories/Pottersfield Press/2022).*

ALISON STEVENSON

Showing

It was months since he'd driven past. The street was part of a series of one-ways leading back where they started; no use pretending he was on his way somewhere. He'd drive by, not even slow down—just glance over and keep going.

He rounded the corner. A sign on the lawn—For Sale, Open House. His brain, untethered, defaulted to habit, guiding the car in a smooth arc past the hedge, into the driveway, behind a Mercedes SUV. He stared ahead, engine idling.

The agent saw the car pull up. She opened the door before the second knock. Tidy jeans, casual shirt, no ring. Quality shoes. He might have a house or condo of his own to sell too. She put on her gracious smile and stepped back to gesture him in, handing him one of the glossy folders. Did he know the neighbourhood?

"I used to know someone around here." His gaze strayed past her towards the living room.

In the kitchen, she pointed out the high-end European appliances. "The owner loves cooking," she said. "She entertains a lot."

His interest was encouraging. Often viewers seemed unimpressed, just going through the motions—no chance of a sale. But he seemed alert, engaged, opening cupboards, checking the fridge, even under the sink. Thank goodness she'd checked the garbage.

Next, the dining room. His attention seemed to dart around, coming to rest on a landscape painting—one of the few owner's pieces the stager had permitted to stay. In the living room, while she pointed out the gas fireplace and the desirable view, he ran a hand along the back of the owner's sofa.

Upstairs, he paused before entering the master bedroom. She demonstrated the window blinds that raised and lowered on a timer. Men were usually fascinated by remote controls. He shifted distractedly.

The walk-in certainly interested him though. Usually, women were more transfixed by the closets, but this *was* a beauty. On the stager's advice, the owner had left enough clothing to make it appear lived-in—an elegant lifestyle any buyer might aspire to, hung on matching hangers an inch apart. On the other side, some of the owner's boyfriend's clothes—an appealing narrative for potential buyers.

The doorbell sounded. Finally—the open house was starting to roll. "Excuse me. I'll let these viewers in and be right back."

The agent's footsteps descended the stairs. Ignoring the men's clothing, he moved towards *her* clothes, the ones she'd chosen for showcasing the house. The chartreuse silk blouse she'd worn that night at the gala. He reached for the cuff and raised it towards his face.

The agent left the new viewers exploring the back yard and went to see if the first viewer had questions. He was gone. Disappointing —he'd seemed genuinely interested. Her instincts were usually reliable—maybe he'd been in a rush, maybe he'd call. Standing in the closet, she had a vague sense something was different, but she couldn't put her finger on what.

Vantage

Deb checked her hair in the ornate mirror, pumped a dollop of expensive-smelling lotion, then paused on the landing, rubbing the scent of lemongrass into her hands. Animated party chatter wafted upstairs, the occasional bray of laughter triggering ripples in response.

At the end of the hallway a door stood open, revealing a corner of plump duvet. The room must look down upon the ravine and the more modest street where she and Christopher lived, in an estate-sale fixer-upper they'd been lucky to get. It was kind of Harry and Monica to invite a new, young couple from the street below and single them out for special attention amongst this older, more-established crowd.

With a glance back towards the stairs, she stepped into the bedroom. Dark treetops in full leaf filled the picture window. Beside it on the dresser lay binoculars; someone must be a birdwatcher. She pictured her hosts on exotic safari—dignified, undeniably wealthy in matching designer khakis.

She couldn't see the backs of the houses below. Christopher had been right, no need for curtains. He liked the bedside lamp on when they did it. "You're lovely, darling. I want to see you."

Beside the window stood a kitchen chair, incongruous amongst the elegant bedroom suite. Deb wondered. She stepped onto the chair and reached for the binoculars. From there she could see that Christopher hadn't turned off the lamp. In the corner, where they sometimes "exercised"—an old joke between them—the exercise ball was clearly visible.

"There you are!" Christopher said when she rejoined him. "Harry and Monica were just inviting us up to their country place. And Harry's generously offered to make some very helpful introductions for my work."

The faces turned towards her. Christopher's expression seemed an excited child's; Harry and Monica's, wolves'.

Moonlight Serenade

The last time the moon was this close was January 26, 1948. On that clear night, sitting on a bench beside the rink, Jane could see how much bigger it was than usual. As she waited, she studied its face gazing down upon her. Later, higher in the sky, it tried to follow her, but became entangled in the strings of lights criss-crossing the ice—the white, round bulbs were almost the same size. But by then he had come and she wasn't thinking of the moon anymore.

She felt his arm around her waist through the layers of sweater and long coat, work clothes underneath. Their laughter intertwined as they wove among the couples circling the rink to the crackling sounds of Glenn Miller's band over the speakers. Colours flashed around her: coats, hats of skaters and onlookers. The waxy ice, bright with reflected light, crunched under their skate blades. Her woollen scarf, beaded with damp breath. Her senses kaleidoscoping in blissful, spinning fragments.

Later as he walked her home, leaving the pool of light and sound behind, the moon was there again. He kissed her.

Years of love and constancy, kindness, quiet joy, loss, grief, and always the moon, distant.

The children are here. They've all come, flickering in and out of her consciousness, even the one who wouldn't wait, who came too soon, too far from help. Low murmurings in the hallway outside her room.

A little while ago the nurse brought some medications and a paper cup of juice for her. She's sleeping now.

The moon comes close, reaching through the window with blue-grey fingers, caressing her hair on the pillow, her paperwhite hands, and gently bathes her face.

Find ***Alison Stevenson's*** *work in* Prairie Fire, The New Quarterly. *Longlisted for CBC and TNQ/Peter Hinchcliffe prizes, finalist in the* Alice Munro Festival Contest. *Alisonstevensonwriter.com*

DANE SWAN

Talking to Myself

In a moment that I would wish never happened in the very near future, my brother and my former co-worker Janice coincidentally left the pub at the same time. The rest of our group slowly left, or made an excuse to sit somewhere else. Amy showed up with a single box and her largest suitcase. Announcing that she couldn't afford her rent, she had decided that she was moving in with me. I think she freaked everybody out. Only Amy would think she could decide to move into a person's place without months of negotiations.

Eventually, I was left staring at her finish off the soup of the day. Her face stained like an enfant terrible wearing a soiled bib. After watching her wipe her face, I placed her suitcase on its wheels, waved to the remaining gang who had huddled in a corner and left, paying our bill at the bar.

It's a fifteen-minute walk to my spot. Despite it getting cold, I decided to walk. Before Amy could complain, I started talking.

—If anyone asks you, I never said what I'm about to say to you. I'm just talking to myself and you happened to overhear. Got it?

I looked to my right and saw a slightly dishevelled five-foot-four woman carrying a box and nodding.

—I don't believe for a second that you're moving in with me to save money. From the way you broke down outside that play last week when I asked how your ex was doing, and the fact no one has heard from him recently, something happened with you guys. Whatever it is, I don't want to know. If I know, and I'm asked, I'm not lying.

—If I got myself caught up in what I suspect you've gotten caught up in, I would lose my cellphone in a public trash can, so that I could say that it got stolen weeks ago. You see that nail place? It's open all night. I would get my nails done, so there's nothing caught in them. When the moving company showed up to put my stuff in storage, I would pay them extra to clean all the furniture, and after I cleared my apartment, I would hire professionals to clean it a second time. Also, I wouldn't hold any emotional attachment to clothes, or shoes. If I thought they needed to be thrown out, I would throw them out.

—If it was me, I would do all of this quietly, and unbeknownst of my partner. That way he could say that I moved in to save money. And when my ex comes up in conversations, I would smile, keep my composure, and leave the breakdowns for closed doors.

—That's what I would do. But this conversation never happened.

I looked at Amy once again. She was staring at me intensely. Hands full, she pressed her shoulder against my side, briefly leaned in to touch my arm with her head and then straightened her posture, as we walked the remaining five minutes in silence.

Dane Swan *is a Toronto-based Black editor and author. His anthology,* Changing the Face of Canadian Literature, *was featured on CBC Books, Best Canadian Books list.*

CANDIE TANAKA

Risotto Interrupted

It was your birthday, so you invited her and your friends over to celebrate. It was just you and her in the kitchen. You were cooking mushroom risotto and as anyone who has cooked risotto knows, it's a delicate process requiring concentration and precise timing. You distractedly talked small talk, then she mentioned her move away into a 1920's apartment which sounded like it had a similar layout to yours, except it's a one bedroom and not a studio.

Then you did that terrible thing that you never do, but you couldn't control yourself and you said with intensity, "You know I am really going to miss you ..." and then you know that piece by John Cage called 4'33? This would have been 8'66, because that's how long the silence lasted. As a friend, couldn't she have even said something like: "Awww, I will miss you too or you should come visit." Instead she said, "But, I am really looking forward to it." With your clumsy recovery skills you chimed in, "But, it will be really good for you, to go back to school."

You've never said that to anyone before, she probably couldn't really care less what you think. But, still there was something hanging in the air between the two of you that seemed like an intense tenderness. You know she felt it too because she wouldn't move from the kitchen. You wanted her to leave because you felt like a big ass fool. Why won't she leave? you thought. Usually she's dashing off somewhere or she's checking her phone for texts from one of the loser guys she is dating. I can't cook this risotto properly, it's fucking starting to stick to the pot bottom, you think, frantically stirring while the liquid reduces itself.

Just then you hear someone yelling your name outside your second floor kitchen window from the side of the building. God, don't these people know that they have these things called buzzers now for apartment buildings? Today, at the most inappropriate time ever, your friends are yelling at you to say they are here.

So, you need help. The risotto needs to be watched because it's at a critical stage and neither you nor her want to leave the kitchen. You ask your wacky friend in the other room entertaining her friend, if she would please let S & her boyfriend in. No response. "Can someone please go downstairs and let them in? I'm cooking the risotto and I can't leave." Finally, she says she will go, thank God, you think but at the same time you don't want her to leave the kitchen.

By the time everyone is back upstairs your friends come to greet you in the kitchen. You have recovered slightly but want them to leave so that the hot girl will come back and just stand near you. You see her motion to but she stops at the entrance because the kitchen is now horribly full.

Leap Year

It's almost the exact same spot that we sat in years ago. Spanish tapas, now a Mexican restaurant. No Manchego and figs, no more marinated olives and crispy chickpeas. Fist-sized burritos, lager on tap and a Tex Mex menu.

I chose the date of February 29th thinking that one day it would mean something to us. Or maybe I knew that there'd eventually be a story for me to write. Nothing huge, but something about the cobblestones in Blood Alley, the new yellow metal chairs and the fresh crowds perhaps.

The server flirted with you, maybe you knew him. They all act as if they know you. Intimately. They definitely want to know you. You were asking about wine. This Leap Year, Adam comes over and introduces himself to me. I order the veggie burrito and a local Vancouver lager.

A painted black unicorn farts out a rainbow on the wall behind the kitchen and I don't know why it's here of all places. After his shift, the Asian cook comes over and sits beside me at the bar. I think he wants me to tell him my story, but I can't because the 80's music is too loud.

I cross the street to the Diamond and order a Last Islander cocktail, Aged Island Rum, Scotch, Citrus and Jamaican Bitters. It tastes like shit. I'm sitting at the same high-top table to the left of the one that we sat at, that night.

If you walked in with your husband …

* * *

This is the second Leap Year that I've waited. The light is glowing soft orange and I'm sitting in a room full of fuzzy warm shadows.

If you walked in alone ...

* * *

The secret room is no longer secret anymore. I wonder if you know this? The wall has been chipped away and there is a diamond shaped entrance to that second bar. The Brazilian server says it happened before she started and that she's only worked here for two and half years. She asks why I'm all dressed up. I have no answer or rather no good answer. I tell her something but it doesn't matter what.

Remember, we were so drunk that we were slipping off the high stools but we kept conversing until after 2 a.m. So drunk that I mistook something you said in the cab for a no. Probably. I didn't realize this until much later. The next day? By then it was too late. I remembered wanting to walk you home instead of taking a cab. I wanted to kiss you in a typical, dark gray and rainy alleyway of Vancouver.

I cap off this evening with the Tiger Breath cocktail, the jalapeno honey makes it sweet and I raise my glass to what could have been us. This is still my favourite bar in Vancouver, but I only visit on February 29th.

Drama Class

Act One

In elementary school I was quite brazen. The first play I ever auditioned for was "A Charlie Brown Christmas." I wanted the lead but I ended up with the part of Lucy. They told me it was because my hair was black like Lucy's and Sarah Porter's was blonde. Those damn blondes.

This other girl, Tracy, was going to play Snoopy because her mom made this amazingly realistic costume with a whole separate dog head and body piece.

I didn't want to wear a dress, instead I insisted upon a purple pantsuit. A much better choice back then. Behind the psychiatric booth I offered help for five cents. I was thrilled to be holding a mic. Nowadays, it seems like I am oftentimes behind that booth again listening to my friends' problems and offering helpful advice.

The part that really stressed me out though was the scene where Snoopy dog kisses Lucy. The famous bit where she screams: "Ugh! I've been kissed by a dog! I have dog germs! Get hot water! Get some disinfectant! Get some Iodine!" Was I going to be kissed by a girl? This would be my first kiss then. The costume saved me though, because the nose was so big that's all that ended up touching my cheek. I can't even remember the name of the girl that kissed me. Later on in life I realized that I should always remember the name of the girl that kisses me.

Act Two

I performed as a magician on stage because I had gone on a road trip to Portland with my parents and had enough money saved for a small magic kit. It included a top hat, magic wand, card tricks, ball and vase, metal linking rings, magic cups with balls and yellow sponge bunnies that I made disappear and reappear. I practiced for days for my performance. It all went pretty smoothly.

Intermission

I loved acting so myself and my friend Katherine (Farmer in the) Dell (I gave her this nickname) would use our lunch hours to write plays so that they would be performed on stage during school assemblies. We were both encouraged by our drama teacher to write and put these shows on.

Closing Scene

I don't exactly know how this happened, but one year I was Santa Claus, I wore my red and white striped Adidas tracksuit, a white elastic dirty gray beard and some black-laced boots. It was like a 70's version of *Bad Santa*. The highlight for me though was when my sixth grade teacher Mrs. Goodheart surprised everyone, and came and sat on my knee. Copious amounts of laughter and shrieking ensued. Ah, Mrs. Goodheart. She would get into trouble nowadays doing something like that.

The little boy in me loved it though and it ruined me for life.

Candie Tanaka *is a multiracial trans writer, an SFU Writer's Studio graduate and has a BFA from Emily Carr University of Art + Design.*

WANDA TAYLOR

Shade Woman

When I walk with them, the length of my shape and the curve of body towers above them. Shading the pair from the sizzle of August's fierce sun. Legs that stretch tall and arms that swing free. Afro hair that shelters like a queen's umbrella. Painted flowers and leaves on coral cotton, wrapped around a worn frame after years of labour and love and loss and life.

They step through the cracks between the sidewalk concrete, reciting the words that echoed from my lips four decades before.

"Step on a crack, break your mother's back."

Like their mother had broken mine, and how I had broken my mother's, and how she had broken her mother's. From worry and fear. From choices and regrets. Broken then repaired, only by the glue of hopes and promises. The ones in their eyes. The ones in their smiles.

Now their thick long curls swing across my path, colourful hair beads jingling and jangling in unison. My shadow is their shade. Protection. They don't stray from it. They check to make sure it's still there.

The wide black photo painted across the cement, moves as they move. Pushes forward against the sudden winds. Shielding and strong.

They don't know that one day this shadow will be replaced with their own, hovering over their own creations—little beings full of new hopes and new promises. But for now, they are content. I am content.

Their arms lock into mine. We are connected at the hand, at the heart, and through the soul. We are forever intertwined among each other's shadows.

Wanda Taylor *is an award-winning author, journalist and educator. She teaches courses in Journalism, Communications, and Storywriting for Media. She lives in Mississauga, Ontario.*

MITCHELL TOEWS

Winter Eve at Walker Creek Park

The three gather, tall and awkward, beside the street. Wide-eyed, they stare at the traffic that streams out of the city centre. A day-long drizzle has just begun to turn to fine snow and they stand back from the curb on the icing-topped grass, partially hidden by a cluster of birch trees.

Streetlights glow in the falling snow and the wet pavement seems to steam.

The tallest of the three is conveniently the oldest too and she studies the cars as if she might know one of the drivers. She tracks each vehicle, her head turning as they pass. Eager to lead a dash across the street, she is restive—waiting for a break in the line.

Richelieu is jammed with shoppers carrying home last minute gifts, food, and bottles of wine. Buses, trucks and taxis compete for space. On the road too are the churchgoers; their minivans loaded with bathrobed wise men and lowing cattle, cozy in their car seats.

Everyone has a place to be that evening.

On slender adolescent legs, vulnerable to the cold, the three sisters walk to the park. Spread like a sheet laid over the brindled openness, the skithed meadows wait for nightime footprints in the darkness beside the bright agitation of the rue.

After crossing the street—lively heels hollow on the pavement—the trio regroups and carries on along the sidewalk, single file. Red taillights light the roadway, snaking down the slope to the intersection below. A few drivers call out to them; others whistle but are ignored.

Reaching a broken section of fence, each in turn steps through the breach, lifting petite legs well above the tangled wire. Close now to their rendezvous they hurry towards the far woods, their destination obscure in the dim light, the illucid snow globe air.

There they are! Shoulders hunched and feet stamping they huddle in the thin copse. Their breath shows in drifting white clouds through the branches as they wait. Narrow, masculine faces and dark eyes are caught in the swinging strobe of headlights from Frontenac Drive as vehicles merge into the moving river of red.

Eyes bright, the three young does hold their heads up to scent the males and then canter, forelegs high across the sleety turf.

Shade Tree Haven

On hot Sundays, I sometimes think of him in his happiest moments at the Tourist Park over in Ste. Anne. The new concrete pool was a cube punched into the mowed grass and filled to the white-tiled rim, the water mirror bright. With our family bakery twenty miles distant—dark and quiet, still until morning—he'd rest in the shade on our picnic blanket. While we kids splashed, he'd sip a beer, pretending to read a paperback novel.

On the hockey rink, he'd been a brick wall, separating the big talkers from their bullshit. No time for that anymore, he was a man and had put aside childish things. Now he toiled in the heat—no number on his back—heaving dough in the hopper, inhaling its yeasty breath, stray puffs of flour tasteless on his lips. Bent over, his rounded fists punched and turned the batch, making our daily bread before the sun rose.

"There was no money in it then," he said once. We were watching the Leafs play some expansion team, St. Louis, maybe. "You either made the NHL or you went home and got a job," he said, staring at the television. He held his glass out to me, rattling the ice. "Refill, kid. Three fingers."

* * *

After a good while in the Sunday shade, he'd get up from his seat against the tree and stretch. Then he'd walk out in the sun and stand on the back of the waiting springboard. With two driving steps, he'd arc up into the most perfect swan dive and pierce the surface like a dart into cork.

When he finished his swim, he'd come back and kneel, facing away from Mom. She'd dry his back with a coarse towel. "I'll *verubble* you!" she'd say, giggling and rubbing so hard with her thin arms that Dad had to steady himself with one hand against the tree trunk. He'd eat a sandwich, grinning eggs and onion bits at us as we tried to mimic his dive. Then it was time for his nap—short legs crossed at the ankles and fingers interlaced on his chest.

"Oh, let him sleep," Mom said, a finger to her lips, when we came running. She lay the *Chatelaine* face down on the blanket, saving her page. I watched her hand rise to remove her sunglasses, then pause as she glanced around quickly. I heard a thin plastic scrape as she unscrewed the lid of a small round jar. It smelled of medicine. Her finger turned powdery beige as she rubbed the cream on below one eye, smearing the make-up caked there. "Just let him sleep," she whispered, replacing her glasses and clasping her bag with a soft click.

Hockey, I think now, closing out the memory as I pull onto our bright driveway after church. *I bet he dreamt of hockey, cold as blue hell.*

Mitchell Toews *is a boreal writer, painter, windsurfer, and rower. He recently released* Pinching Zwieback – Prairie Stories, *a short fiction collection (At Bay Press).*

AYELET TSABARI

Moonstruck

Once, on a sandy beach in southern India, I met a German woman whose name I can't recall. She was a petite woman with glassy blue eyes and black hair that smelled of coconut oil. She lived with her son in a little house at the end of the beach, past a coconut grove and near a fresh water lake where I used to wash the salt off after swimming in the sea. Every afternoon when the local school bell rang, and students in uniform swarmed the village's streets, I could spot her son, a single blonde dot in a swirling river of black-haired heads.

One night at a party she told me that as a young woman in Hamburg she was obsessed with the moon. "I was younger then, maybe your age," she said. "I used to stare at it for hours. I followed it when I was in a car or a train. I couldn't take my eyes off it! And on nights with no moon I felt restless."

"Moonstruck," I said.

"Yes!" she exclaimed, raising her glass in agreement. "Moonstruck! I did everything but howl at it." She burst into a big laugh. She had the habit of laughing at her own jokes and you couldn't help joining in.

"Well," I said, repeating something a friend once told me, "if the moon affects something as big as the sea, no wonder it affects us."

"Well put." She nodded into her wine glass.

It was a full moon night and the party was at its peak. People mingled and flirted, fresh fish grilled on the open fire, the smell of cashew blossoms sweetened the salty breeze, and the night air was sticky and moist—like sex. The German woman was elated and tipsy and in good company. She laughed like a woman in love.

I went to get a beer and when I came back she was already engaged in another lively conversation with an older Russian man named Siddhartha who had been giving me dirty looks all night long. I interrupted. "What happened then?" I said.

She turned to me, her eyebrows raised in surprise. "What happened *when*?"

"With the moon," I said. "Why did you stop?"

She shrugged. "Oh, I don't know. I had my son. I guess I found better things to do than stare at the moon."

She laughed and everyone around joined in. I was going to tell her that I too was once obsessed with the moon, that when I was little I used to see my father's face in it, but now she was laughing about something else, her cheeks flushed red and her eyes shiny, and I couldn't bear to bring up dead fathers and ruin the moment.

The moon walked me back to the guesthouse, fat and white, his smile thin and content. The coconuts on the trees glistened in his fluorescent light.

Sleeping Outdoors

He built a tent from two sarongs and three sticks. It covered about half of their bodies when they lay down straight. Their calves were showing.

"This is great!" she lied, looking up at the tie-dye sarong stretched between the wooden sticks. When she stretched her head back she saw a row of straw huts between palm trees, and flickering candles lighting up the only restaurant on the beach. Their arms were touching. She was afraid to move.

"Wanna sleep here tonight?" he asked, and she said, and really tried to mean it: "Yeah, totally!"

He was twenty-one and she was thirty. She was on vacation. Her parents thought it would be good for her to clear her head after everything she'd gone through. They even helped paid for it. He's been travelling for a while, a small backpack, a drum and a didgeridoo. He smoked local cigarettes and smelled like smoked salted fish. He rarely showered, his skin felt like sand paper when she caressed him. Once, in the forest, he pulled out his knife, cracked open a coconut and put it to her mouth; thin white juice dripped on her chin when she drank it. Then he carved her a smiley face on the shell.

Truth was she didn't like sleeping outdoors. She had rented an air conditioned hotel room most backpackers couldn't afford. She didn't take him to her hotel room, embarrassed by her private bathroom, the beauty products she had arranged in a neat row on the sink. She had even brought her blow dryer.

In the middle of the night, it started to rain, and then she wasn't on the beach, but in water, drowning. The water was dark and she didn't see a shore. When she opened her mouth to call for help, she found herself calling his name. She was swallowing water, gulps of thick black oil. She started to choke.

"Relax," she said aloud. She read somewhere that people drown because they panic, and so they start kicking and flailing like a spider in a sink and they waste all their energy and die. She floated on her back and breathed deep through her nose. Her body became lighter until she was a leaf surfing in a stream of rainwater. When she finds him, she decided, she will tell him. "I'm in love with you," she'll say. "I don't want anything from you; I just want to be honest about it."

When she woke up she saw the tide had risen and water covered their feet. He was curled into a ball, like a kid, snoring lightly. She touched his shoulder, it was sandy and warm, like a seashell on the beach in midday. She stood up and went back to her room.

Ayelet Tsabari *is the author of* The Art of Leaving, *winner of the Canadian Jewish Literary Award for Memoir, and* The Best Place on Earth.

EMILY UTTER

Burn Barrel

I come from a long line of women who compose letters in their heads. Women who bite back then swallow whole the things they want to say. We do not like confrontation—prefer to play back an episode of discomfort or disagreement later, in the shower maybe, when we can imagine we had all the power.

We suffer from trembles and migraines and bellyaches. When we swallow our words they travel through us, trying to break out in other ways—through the skin like sweat. Sometimes the words go to our wombs and take our babies, other times they bubble up as tumours that grow, then shrink, then kill us anyway.

I spit out my words so they don't make me sick. Tell my brother he is being an idiot. Tell the dog he is being a toenail. Tell Dad he doesn't know *everything* and Mum that I will *not* practice piano. When Joe, the farm hand, tries to tell me what to do I remind him that I don't have to because my Dad is the boss. Loudly announce to anyone who will listen that I'm a boy so I don't have to wear a shirt if I don't want to.

My grandma is so old and has had time to swallow so many words that she can't keep hold of them anymore. They clog up her brain then spill out of her mouth and she calls my dad five different names before she finally lands on his.

It doesn't matter, he'll respond to any of them. Dad doesn't soak in words like the rest of us. Instead of swallowing his words Dad gathers up the spare junk in the farmyard, rotting chicken carcasses the raccoons have abandoned, and split 6-quart baskets, then lights up a fire in the burn barrel. He'll stand there for hours, stoking the embers, then bringing the flames back up to a roar with a bit of pitch pine.

When he comes back to the house he stinks of smoke and his face is drawn but we know his belly is aching with hunger, not words, because he cracks a beer and says, 'starvin' Marvin,' as he leans over whatever is bubbling on the stove.

Lately I've been dreaming of a fire raging through the orchards, smothering the sky in black smoke, and sucking everything—the trees, the house, the barn—up as it goes.

Eggs

It was the year we left the farm. The year the pond dried up and the land cracked and the one last attempt to yield something from it—didn't. The chickens died from drinking the brackish ground water and we bought our eggs at the store. They were never fresh, and that whole year we ate them boiled because Mum said it was all they were good for.

It was the year I got braces, cracked lips. Lost that extra bit of baby fat and got cat-called on the way to lunch by the boys in grade twelve. I hardly noticed when Mum had the kitchen walls re-papered because, that spring, all the local farm kids started hosting barn parties and every weekend I went out hoping to have my first kiss. One night, my friend Caroline drank too much and barfed in my dad's truck. The next day, Mum told her she had to fess up but she never did because her parents were Baptists and she was supposed to be dating God.

It was the year my parents finally reached a settlement with the landfill across the road. Boxes arrived, got filled, and I tore the heads off all my old Barbies so that they had to go in the trash. For some reason, I didn't want to donate them. Didn't want other kids playing with my things. I left for camp the day before we moved and missed the whole shebang—did not, like my younger brother, have to sleep on the blow up mattress on Grandma's floor. Vibrating and slick with the Southern Ontario heat, I unravelled my new red polka-dot bikini from my pack and thought nothing of my family, far away, unpacking boxes, shucking eggs.

The Body

When they found the body I went down to the edge of the escarpment to watch. I knew he was naked except for a pair of black sneakers because I'd seen him weeks earlier, out for what Dad called a 'nature dander.'

From where I stood I could just see his bare legs stretched out, like his heart had stopped in the middle of him making a snow angel. Except it was May and there hadn't been any snow for months. It wasn't the cold that killed him.

I didn't know for a long time what had happened to him. All I have to go on is what Mum told me: apparently, he'd gone out there to die because he was very sick and that was the best way to go.

People go into the woods—into national parks like Yosemite—and keep walking until they succumb to the elements or die of hunger or thirst. Or else they die of whatever it was that made them go out there in the first place.

I understood that inclination to be alone, to be gone so long that someone might come looking for me. How many times had I wandered out on the farm and tried to get lost? Turned myself around in the trees and walked backwards trying to disorientate myself.

You can't get lost in a place you know—not like the back of your hand—like the smell of Mum and Dad's sheets when you've got the flu and their bed is the best place to recuperate.

I remember that day we saw him. Even though we hadn't known it at the time, it was the last walk we took together down on the farm. It was a bluebird day, spring well on its way, and something hopeful in the air. At least, I don't remember any of us feeling sad or angry.

"Don't look!" Dad flapped his hands at Mum and me. We were giggling and pawing at the trees, trying to get a better view.

"What's he doing?"

"He's out there being one with nature."

"He's on farm property," I said.

Dad shrugged.

We watched him for less than a minute. For the first time I felt I was trespassing on someone else. I looked around as we picked our way back to the laneway: no cars driving in unannounced, no kids from pick-your-own scrambling all over my swing set, no members of the Men's Club to be spied on while they drank Coors Light in the cold storage, no satellite dishes that beckoned aliens, no lawyers at the door. No moving vans, yet.

The sun shone through the gnarled remains of Dad's cherry trees and tiny beadlets of dew clung to the tall grasses.

It was quiet—except for a shallow gulp of barn swallows. They swooped and dove down in front and behind us, snatching up bugs, ushering us along.

I think it was morning. There was still a whole day ahead of us.

She Did Not Leave

Not through the bathroom window, which was open, not through the front door, which was unlocked. She did not leave, even though her mother, sister, co-worker had told her that she should.

She could not leave, could not peel her feet from the wet tile or her back from the wall, even though the sky outside was clear and cloudless and the sun was a shining beacon of, if not hope, then clarity.

She would not leave even though the house was damp and dark. She would not lift her eyes from the empty beer bottle on the edge of the bath to see the remnants of an erupted lip on the mirror.

Tiny red dots, a smudge like a thumb. She fogs up the glass with warm breath and uses a scrunched ply of toilet paper to wipe it all away.

'Just the dog,' she rehearses. 'Jumped up and got me in the mouth.'

Silver Chest

The silver chest overflows—not with butter spreaders (there are four), or mustard spoons (there are six), which is quite something because the set was at one time split, but with certificates of authenticity, receipts so ancient they are transparent, and with prophetic lettering on dated post-it notes and bits of paper torn from notepads that read 'Midnight Cove: Sarasota.'

I trace her words—they look so like my mother's—with the tip of my finger, trying to lift a memory up out of the ink. She signs her notes with 'J' instead of Mum.

'For Susie Mary—a little elegance for my first-born. Perhaps it will last for your first-born too.' It's dated April '86—almost two years before I came into this world screaming and a girl.

Silver does not get passed down to sons, to brothers. They cannot carry, do not feel the weight of twelve knives, forks, spoons, the same way that daughters do.

Emily Utter *is a Canadian prose writer based in Scotland. She is a palliative care writer-in-residence and teaches creative writing at the local college.*

LYNDA WILDE

Taking The Measure

A woman is crossing a parking lot to her car, her arms around a brown bag holding bottles of wine. As she approaches she looks up to see a man standing between her car and a brick wall as if waiting for her. *Could you give me some money?* He is stocky, wears jeans and a faded windbreaker, one knee bent up so that the sole of his boot rests against the wall. His hands move around in his pockets. She avoids his glance, looks down into the bag and then off to the side where two crows are standing on the roof of a car, getting ready to outwit a seagull. The woman has only a credit card in the pocket of her own jeans. She looks back at the man, takes the measure of him. The seagull is nearing a hunk of bread on the pavement. One crow flies to his side and distracts him. The other swoops down, grabs the bread, and the pair fly away together.

The woman opens her car and finds a bill. *Thanks* the stranger says and now she looks at him more directly.

What are you going to do with it?

Buy a drink.

Good, she thinks. *You look like you need a stiff one.*

The seagull is bewildered, walks round in circles.

The Bend In The Road

There's a great bend in the road that leads to San Marcos Tlapazola. From the vantage point of the vulture, high up in the thermals, the road is a white line tracking through fields of green agave toward a lone acacia tree. At the tree the road takes a turn west toward the foothills of the Sierra Madre and the distant pueblo.

She always slows at the bend to have full view of the tree before rounding the curve. *That is where I want my ashes spread.* Friends take note and nod. *That is the spot*, and they drive on to the rugged little town and buy red pottery from the women there.

* * *

She walks through the field of green agave, small clouds of red dust trailing her, and places a weary hand on the trunk of the old acacia. The road has been widened and so the tree is now closer to the great bend, and with further widening, there may not be a tree.

But it is here now and will be when they come with the ashes. She wants to feel steady with that thought. She watches the vulture circle against the intense blue of the sky, then looks across the gentle slope of the valley with its *milpas*, toward Oaxaca, tries hard not to forget the old city.

She lived in Mexico for many winters, happy to abandon ice and snow, forever. She was never at home in the northern cold, even as a child. But neither did she harbour illusions of being at home in Mexico. She knew she was an outsider, a *güerita*.

This does not lessen her attachment to the place or to her fading desire to linger near the tree.

How much time in this dry breeze and shade?

How long to register the pueblo in thc foothills or the shadow of the vulture crossing the *milpa*?

How long to recall that small serious child who was so suddenly old?

The Juggler

There is a young woman at a busy street corner. She wears the traditional cotton skirt and huipil of her pueblo and has a baby tied to her back with an old purple cloth. There are two small boys in jeans and tee shirts. The youngest is seated, chin on knees, near a large sawed off stump in the median they occupy between the relentless streams of traffic. The oldest, perhaps four, stands on the stump. When the light turns yellow and the traffic slows, the mother turns her back to him, bends down a bit and the little boy climbs and stands on her shoulders. He has a coloured ball in each hand, one blue, one yellow. With one hand gripping his ankle and the other a plastic cup, the mother steps out amid the vehicles and the boy begins to throw the balls up in the air like a juggler. The baby is visible only as a lump beneath the purple cloth. The child left behind on the median watches patiently as his mother negotiates the traffic. The grime on his skin and clothes appear to weigh him down. The juggler seems to be having fun tossing the balls in the air with success. He is good at what he does and has already learned to please a crowd. He is the star of the show. Who taught him this skill, an uncle in the pueblo on warm evenings? Or has his mother thought up the scheme and trained him, encouraged him on the bus each morning on their way to the thronging city? Her young eyes are already dimmed with the weight of her task. How to feed this family of four with a few pesos earned in the thick of traffic, her oldest juggling, day after hot Mexican day.

Other Person

I once lived for a week with a household of Buddhist nuns in an old stucco dwelling amid vineyards in the south of France. On my first day I was assigned 'another person' to keep an eye on. One did not have to be acquainted with one's other person or even like her. It was simply a way of keeping track of people without that responsibility falling to one person. There was no headcount at meals or meditation. So, if you had not seen your other person for a while you were expected to report to the head nun. I rather liked the concept of having responsibility for a stranger. My short stay in the mostly silent community offered scant chance of acquaintance. I had no idea whose other person I was and wondered, if I paid close attention (their practice) could I figure it out? I also wondered if the system was in place out of genuine concern, or had they been caught out? Had someone been left suffering in this place of purposeful compassion?

Through The Glass

There is a time of year when the lake goes green, the opaque green of pale jade. In late afternoon the sun washes the green wind-blown surface with a layer of pearl. These are the dog days, the days you forget until summer slows and you recall again that it will end. The great lake is finally warm enough for swimming. Soon pickerel will run beneath the moon, old loves will occupy the mind, and for a brief time you will forget that there is any other kind of day but this one. I thought I saw you again today, the clothes, the gait, the person you were. I strained to see through the glass but light bounced off the lake and I was pushed on by traffic. I adjusted the rear view mirror, tried once more for a glimpse of you.

Lynda Wilde *is a Canadian writer/photographer who lives between the cities of Kingston, Ontario, Canada, and Oaxaca de Juárez, Mexico, when not travelling elsewhere.*

K.R. WILSON

Immortality

The most fundamentally important thing—more important than trading the dwindling books for electrical power or gathering raw materials for food or teaching the young their letters—was maintaining the Transfigurator. Books and letters were just knowledge and commerce. The Transfigurator was existence.

Like all youth, ShaSha had been trained in transfiguration as part of her schooling. It had been clear early on that she was gifted. In her cohort's final test—where most students turned their assigned bales of grasses and leaves into plain protein nuggets or porridges—ShaSha had produced five bright spheres that, according to the elders who remembered that far back, had the taste and texture of actual apples. As a reward, she'd been allowed to keep one. Most youth in her position would have eaten it. She'd taken it to Artor.

He'd been in his usual spot in the scriptorium, supervising the hand-copying of the books. Even then, twelve seasons ago, his teeth hadn't been up to biting through the apple's taut green skin, so she'd carved thin, juicy slices for him out on the balcony, and he'd eaten them with his eyes closed, smiling.

"Very much the way I remember them," he'd said. "Though a classic apple would have had a stem, from its connection to the tree, and a fibrous bit in the middle full of seeds for regeneration."

"I thought about including those," ShaSha had replied. "But they seemed wasteful. And the seeds would've been sterile."

"They could've gone back into the machine, for the next creation."

"True. But this way they go into you. For your next creation."

And he'd smiled again. "Very thoughtful. Maybe I'll write something about apples, then. Bring it full circle." Artor was the one who wrote the stories. Not the only one, but the best. In ShaSha's mind at least.

That had been when there was still paper, in boxes, in storage. When writing and copying—for their own community and for trade—were well resourced. Before Artor and his scribes had been reduced to cannibalizing blank pages from the ends of pre-existing books, and then to bleaching pages from books the council decided were inferior.

Now Artor was gone, and so was the paper. Without paper, the remaining books would soon be lost to trade, leaving the community without its recorded knowledge. And with nothing to trade to power the Transfigurator.

The council didn't like ShaSha's idea at first. Some said it violated the rule against processing the dead into food. In spirit, at least. But eventually she persuaded them.

They gowned Artor in white and lay him in the Transfigurator's input chamber. The whole council attended. No one had ever done anything like this. By the end, ShaSha's muscles ached and she was drenched in sweat. But it had worked.

The output chamber was filled to its top with clean, blank sheets of paper.

When writers die they become books
which is after all not too bad an incarnation.
—Jorge Luis Borges

K. R. Wilson *is the author of the novels* An Idea About My Dead Uncle *(Guernica Prize 2018) and* Call Me Stan. *He lives in Toronto.*

EDITORS' PREROGATIVE

BRUCE MEYER

Family

She greeted me with a hug on the pier in New York City. The last time I'd seen Clara I was a child of five and she was blond and about to marry Saul. My father and Clara had the same light in their smiling green eyes. They looked so much alike anyone could tell she was his daughter.

When the Germans came to our village they gathered the men and shot them behind the blacksmith's shop. Women who ran out to find their husbands and sons were herded onto trucks. My mother knew I was hiding under our shed but she did not turn or wave goodbye. That would have given me away. I never saw her again.

After the war, the Red Cross claimed they'd located my sister but when I arrived the wrong Clara met me. The woman in New York was taller and had black hair. She had brown eyes. What did it matter? Out of fear I accepted the stranger's kindness. I thought I remembered my sister's eyes like my father's but the details blurred over the years.

The American Clara gave me a good life. I was all she had. I wept when she breathed her last.

I never found my real sister. Too much time had passed. Strife chews up families but time swallows them. So what is a family? Can anyone say? My sister, Clara, if she survived as the other Clara had, she probably lost the light in her green eyes.

The Boiling Point

Gwen stared out the window at the blizzard and waited for the courier to come with Maggie's precious metformin pills. She thought about the trail dogs that once ran to deliver medicine to remote communities such as hers and was reminded of the name of the first encyclopedist. Iditarod. Diderot.

Moving here from the city had been Dave's idea. The telephone company needed linemen, and they offered to double his pay.

Thin wires of conversation stretched along the old logging roads and hydro clear cuts. She had been playing tin-can telephone with Mags on a morning like this when she received word that Dave had slipped and fallen from a repeater station early the night before. He had lain in the snow through long lonely hours, his cellphone useless because he had shut down the tower to repair it. The weather gradually crept inside him, leaving a starry patch among the snow-laden pines and silence on his phone.

One very cold day when Gwen was eight, her mother put a pot on the stove to boil. She called the girls into the kitchen as steam clouds rose. "Open the back door!" she exclaimed. "I'm going to show you a miracle!" With the door wide open, Gwen had felt the deep chill wrap its arms around her. Her mother took the pot and flung the contents into the air. In an instant, the scalding liquid became snow.

Mags walked into the kitchen in her sleepers. Her face was grey, and her forehead was covered in beads of cold sweat. The mother and daughter exchanged glances that betrayed the fact that both knew, almost instinctively, that the situation was growing direr by the minute.

A pot of hot water that Gwen had put on for tea was mumbling on the stove.

"Let me show you something," Gwen said, trying to cheer her child. She grabbed the pot from the burner and set it momentarily on the countertop beside the kitchen door. With a push, she was able to force the door over the newly stacked snow that tried to bar her inside the house. Mags approached cautiously as Gwen picked up the pot of steaming water.

"Watch," she said to the child. "Mommy is going to make magic." The air, as she breathed in, hardened inside her nose to the point that she could almost feel her head crack. She flung the water into the air above the small porch, and instantly it became a reeling cloud of steam.

Mags gasped and Gwen dropped the empty pot as Dave's pale shadow appeared in the sudden whir of snowflakes, his hands empty and reaching out to them.

MICHAEL MIROLLA

The Main Road

I am coming down an escalator when I suddenly turn around and run back up against the moving steps. I seem to have forgotten something in the room I've just left. It appears to be a lecture hall or reading space of some sort, with chairs lined up and facing a podium. I search all the chairs one by one, going up and down the rows. But there's nothing there. And no one to ask. I take the escalator again and come out the side of the building onto the street. A plaza really with streets leading off it. I don't recognize the plaza or the streets. I do know I need to take a bus or subway as I live a long way off. I reach into my pockets for money or tokens and don't find any. Maybe I can call a friend to come and pick me up. I pull out a cell phone. It appears to be old and scruffy, all scratched up. I hold down the power button but nothing happens. I will have to walk home. But first I have to get onto a main road that I can identify. Some way to orient myself. I start to walk, knowing that sooner or later I'll come upon that road that will allow me to head home. But the first street, along a series of buildings that resemble factories but which are inhabited, becomes more and more narrow—until it ends in a backyard filled with bicycle parts and scruffy patches and tufts of grey-coloured grass. I try to see beyond to determine if perhaps I can slip through the backyard and onto the next street. But the houses are crammed together and I don't see any streets or even alleys. This happens half a dozen times, the street leading to homes whose backyards are filled with all kinds of junk—from automobile frames to pieces of derricks and oil rigs, from smashed old-style TV sets to rusted out lawn chairs. In frustration, I decide to take a shortcut through one of these homes. I step out onto a patio where a group of people are enjoying themselves around a barbecue. They make laughing noises and seem quite at ease. I look out and find myself surrounded by never-ending fields. In the distance, a slow wide river from which steam rises. On the other bank, a temple of some sort: round and squat with perforated grey stone, making it look like a giant brain. I ask one of the guests how I can get on a main road from here. He shrugs and begins to tell me about the land and those who own it and the others who could show me the main road because he can't, not knowing a main road from a muddy path. I continue to look out, a queasy feeling rising, knowing that the road is out there.

Again at the Ministry

A pale, thin, tubercular-looking young man wearing rimless glasses sits in the corner taking notes. He seems strangely familiar with his sharp nose and sunken cheek bones. A bank clerk perhaps or insurance-claims agent. All about him, dishevelled files have been stacked, some so high they slide to the ground and spill out their contents—only to be all jumbled together during the next clean-up. I hold my credentials tightly in my hand: a contract with the State Government offering me a teaching position and re-enforced by a letter of posting. Young men in high-heeled shoes and gaudily-checked bellbottoms bustle about, carrying messages and files. Or they wait barely out of sight, somnambulant, lids half-shut, mouths half-open, the flies circling for an opportunity. The clerk-agent in the corner coughs (definitely tuberculosis, I find myself thinking). Dust rises from the spilled files, from the desks, from the shoes. Everyone speaks a strange, guttural language that sounds like the cracking of walnuts. They laugh and play jokes on one another, especially the women who talk as if the words have to be pulled out of them. After waiting an hour, I am led to a desk where an important-looking official sits. I know he is important from the large bowl of tea and biscuits before him. My problem will be solved at last.

—Are you the Permanent-Secretary? I ask.

At this, the entire office bursts into uncontrolled laughter. Even the clerk-agent in the corner looks up momentarily from his files to offer a slight grin.

—No. But this is the closest you'll get to him today. Now, what can I do for you?

I explain that I have been waiting more than a month to be posted, that my wife and child are tired of living in a hotel, that ... He smiles, holds up a finger to cut me off, and hands me a form. Then he tells me to see the Accountant. One of the high-heeled young men turns to inform him the Accountant isn't in. Something about his aunt. Everyone laughs again.

—Please come back another time, the pseudo-Permanent Secretary says with a shrug. We'll fix you up then, I'm sure.

From past experience, I know there is no point in insisting. And it is only while I am well on my way back to the hotel that I finally remember who that young clerk-agent in the corner is.

Acknowledgements

Dessa Bayrock's "The Patron Saint of Butchers is also the Patron Saint of Surgeons and Abortions" appeared previously in *PRISM* magazine (Fall 2019).

John Blair's "Morder" appeared previously online in *LiteraryYard.com* (February 28, 2021).

Larry Brown's "Flintstones" appeared previously in *Montana Mouthful* (Issue 2, 2019).

Mary King's "The Roaring Twenties" appeared previously in *filling Station* (Issue 77, 2021).

Bruce Meyer's "The Boiling Point" appeared previously in *A Chronicle of Magpies* (Tightrope Books, 2014).

Ellie Presner's "Stung" appeared previously in *formercactus* (Issue Four), an online magazine of prose, poetry, and art.

Karen Schauber's "A Real Doll" appeared previously in *Across the Margin* (2019); "Sarabande" previously appeared in *The Blake-Jones Review* (2020).

Mitchell Toews' "Winter Eve at Walker Creek Park" appeared previously in *CommuterLit.com* as "Winter Eve at Walker Creek" (February 17, 2017); "Shade Tree Haven" appeared previously in *macromic.org* (November 29, 2019).

About the Editors

Bruce Meyer *is the author of 69 books of short stories, flash fiction, poetry, and non-fiction. His stories and flashes have won numerous national and international prizes, the most recent of which is the Editor's Commendation from the Scottish Arts Flash Fiction Competition. His previous work of flash fiction is* Down in the Ground *(Guernica Editions, 2020). He lives in Barrie, Ontario and teaches at Georgian College.*

Michael Mirolla's *publications include three Bressani Prize winners: the novel* Berlin*; the poetry collection* The House on 14th Avenue*; and the short story collection* Lessons in Relationship Dyads. *His novella,* The Last News Vendor, *won the 2020 Hamilton Literary Award for fiction. Two short stories – "The Sand Flea" and "Casebook: In The Matter of Father Dante Lazaro" – are Pushcart Prize nominees. Michael calls Hamilton, Ontario home.*

Printed in June 2022
by Gauvin Press,
Gatineau, Québec